THE

PATHOGEN

The Pathogen

ISBN: 0-9759240-7-9

Library of Congress Control Number: 2004095037

Manufactured in the United States of America
South Beach Publishing Company
5059 Newport Avenue Ste.106
San Diego, CA

At last her office building came into sight. As the bus approached it Emily moved to the front exit and said to the driver,

"Stop right here."

"This isn't a taxi lady. We only stop at bus stops."

To the consternation of Emily the bus whizzed on for another block. The driver pulled over but a parked car partially encroached on the bus stop, and the bus stopped two feet from the curb.

Emily leaped for the sidewalk, but the heel of her right shoe caught on the lip of the curb; she hit the pavement. The palms of her hands were scraped; pain in her left knee; she looked down to see her hose torn and her knee abraded and bleeding.

Without a look back the bus driver put the bus into gear and took off.

Her skirt was soiled with sidewalk dust and, looking into the gutter she saw her right shoe.

"Damn it!" Emily thought, "I'm already late for the meeting, and now this."

Emily thanked the Good Samaritan who had helped her up; she picked up her shoe from the gutter and put it on. She picked up her computer case and started off toward her office building. But her shoe was wobbling back and forth each time it was asked to support her weight. She looked down and saw that the heel of the shoe was bent about thirty degrees out of shape. Emily stopped, slipped off both shoes and went on in stocking feet.

A wide wooden walkway over an ornamental pool led to the front entry of her office building. Emily pulled open one of the two glass doors and entered the lobby.

The floor and the walls of the lobby were of beige-colored marble tile; there was a high, vaulted ceiling; and above, three enormous crystal chandeliers, their myriad of tiny lights contributing a diamond reflection to the crystals of the chandelier. Each of the three elevator doors was paneled in satin gold metal.

Emily had never been in the lobby. She had always parked her car in the underground garage and then took the elevator to her fourteenth floor office. She brought lunch with her and ate in the Board Room.

The phrase, 'Board Room' was a kind of joke. To begin with they had no Board. There were only four employees. Mr. Andrews was the boss, Mary Ann, the receptionist, and Petie, was Emily's assistant. "Petie!" She had forgotten to phone Petie; Petie was at home sick with the flu. She would call her after the meeting and stop by her apartment later to see if she was O.K.

The Board Room was about the size of the average living room. Furniture consisted of a large mahogany table, with two upholstered arm chairs at each side and one at each end; light, gray-beige carpeting covered the floor and the lower half of the walls were paneled in mahogany.

There was a small half partition in one corner of the room and this screened off a coffee maker and a small refrigerator. The room was used almost exclusively as a lunch room for the employees.

When the elevator door opened Emily headed for the ladies washroom. She washed her hands and her bruised knee, brushed the street dirt from the skirt of her black suit. She checked in the mirror, wiped a smudge from her nose and, with a twist of her head, gave a swirl to her straight, shoulder-length, blonde hair. Her flawless blue eyes approved. She took a deep breath and headed for the office.

"I'm sorry I'm late," she rehearsed, "I had a flat tire and . . . no, that sounds phony, just say, "I'm sorry I'm late," she could explain later to Mr. Andrews what had happened.

A man was approaching in the hallway; medium height, rather slender, with high cheek bones, a pencil mustache and sallow skin. He wore a black slouch hat and dark glasses. He seemed to be heading for the stairway at the end of the hall but just then the elevator door opened and a woman left the elevator. Seeing the open elevator the man made an abrupt turn, entered the elevator. The elevator doors closed.

The lettering on the glass entry door of Emily's office said, "GENERIC RESEARCH INC.," which didn't give much of a clue as to the business activities engaged in. Below was the office number, "1420." Mary Ann was not at her receptionist desk; they must have called her into the meeting.

Emily stopped at the Board Room door, put on her shoes and straightened her skirt. If she held her computer case in front of her, perhaps they wouldn't notice her damaged knee.

She pushed the door open and said, " I'm sorry I'm . . ."

That was as far as she got. In front of her, Mary Ann was lying face down on the floor with a crimson splotch on the back of her white blouse. Blood had oozed out onto the carpeting beneath her. Mr. Andrews, seated with his back to the entry door, had collapsed forward with his head on the table. On his right, Candejar from their Mexico operation, had fallen backward and was in a sitting position on the floor, with his back against the wall. He had a bullet hole in his forehead. His chair had been pushed backward; he was probably standing when he was shot.

On the left of Andrews, the two men visiting from Colombia were slouched in their chairs, one to the left and the other to the right as though they were leaning on each other, blood on their faces and clothing. Emily's thoughts swirled through her head like evil spirits over which she had no control. And then their message became clear. "They are all dead!"

Emily backed out of the room; she wanted to scream but brought forth only choking gasps. Kicking off her shoes in panic she turned and ran; in the outer hall she pressed the elevator button and waited; her breath came in gasps; her hands trembled. The elevator door opened. She stared at the space before her. There was no one in the elevator, there was no one in the hallway. She turned; there was no one in the office; no one was pursuing her.

Her trembling stopped, her breathing slowed; the panic attack was over and she knew what she had to do.

At the receptionist desk Emily picked up the telephone. From her wallet she retrieved a small slip of paper on which was printed the name, ARMITAGE, with a telephone number. She dialed; when a secretary answered she said, "Mr. Armitage, emergency!"

A few seconds later male voice said, "Armitage."

"This is Emily Smith in Los Angeles." This was the first she had spoken since viewing the grizzly scene but she made herself speak calmly.

"They've all been killed." With a shudder Emily described the scene.

Armitage said, “I’ll call the FBI. You call the police. Don’t tell the police anything but you’ll have to level with the FBI.” He paused, “Do I have your cell number?"

"Yes."

"All right, I'll be in touch with you tomorrow," and he hung up.

“He doesn’t waste any words,” Emily thought.

She dialed nine-one-one. When the operator answered she said. "Some people have been shot."

II

Sergeant Burris was a man you could dislike before he even opened his mouth. He was a large man, over six feet in height with flat, broad shoulders. His brush-style haircut gave his head a squarish look, and his thick neck was just a downward extension of his head. A flat triangular nose with bulky, flaccid, facial features suggested that Burris was not only past his prime, but that he took no active part in slowing its decline. His pale, yellow-green eyes were capped with almost invisible eyebrows. His clothing, although clean, looked unpressed.

Burris, with his back to the waiting room wall, sat facing Emily. His partner, Detective Johnson, sat to Emily's right.

"Tell us what happened," Burris said.

"I was late for the meeting; my car had a flat tire and . . ." The detectives exchanged glances. "I went directly to the washroom because I slipped and fell when I was getting off the bus, and my hands and skirt were dirty; my stocking was torn." She didn't mention that she had broken the heel in her right shoe.

It all sounded so stupid. "They must think I'm some kind of looney," Emily thought.

A police officer leaned over and whispered something to Detective Johnson. Johnson got up and left with the officer.

"Did you know all of the people who were at the meeting?" Burris asked.

"No, just Mr. Andrews and Mr. Candejar and Mary Ann. Mary Ann wasn't part of the meeting, she was our receptionist and secretary; they must have called her into the meeting for some reason."

Burris asked, "What was the purpose of the meeting?"

Armitage had instructed her not to tell the local police anything. Emily tried to think of an evasive answer but she couldn't . In reply to the question she said, "It was a private meeting."

Emily detected twitch of the eyes but the detective said nothing; she continued,

"Two of the men were Colombians, I didn't know their names."

"Why were the Colombians at the meeting?"

Emily didn't want to lie so she said, "I can't tell you that."

Burris leaned forward till their faces were only inches apart. His voice was quiet and steady but his pale, yellow-green eyes held a threat. His thin lips parted in what was intended as a smile, but only revealed his yellowed teeth and gave him an even less attractive appearance.

"This is a murder investigation, lady. There are severe penalties for withholding information. It's referred to as Obstruction of Justice."

Emily very slowly raised her chin, turned her head slightly to her right and lowered her eyelids, all the time keeping her eyes fixed on Burris. Burris tried to stare her down, but Emily didn't blink.

The detective was distracted; something was happening at the entry door to the office. When Emily looked over her shoulder to follow the detective's gaze she saw Detective Johnson talking to two men. Both wore dark-gray pinstripe suits. Emily guessed who they were and let out a little gasp of relief.

Johnson left the two men at the door, approached Burris, leaned over, nodded his head toward the door and said quietly, "FBI."

Burris growled something incomprehensible, rose, and without excusing himself, lumbered over to the entry accompanied by Johnson. While Burris talked to one of the FBI men the second approached with Detective Johnson.

Emily rose and turned to meet him; she didn't like the chair she had been sitting in, facing the wall, and with her back to the waiting room area.

Johnson said, "This is Special Agent Musgrove of the FBI;" and to Musgrove, "This is Emily Smith."

Emily extended a slender hand, "How do you do."

Musgrove smiled, gave the hand a careful shake, showed his FBI identification and said, "I'm pleased to meet you." He nodded to Johnson and Johnson, correctly interpreting the nod, excused himself and left.

Musgrove complied with the stereotype image that Emily had of FBI agents. He was middle aged, probably in his early fifties, with blue eyes, light brown hair and a nicely tanned complexion. His hair was parted on his left, neatly trimmed, not too long and not too short. His gray pinstripe suit was of a fine wool worsted, expensive. A neatly patterned tie on a light-gray shirt completed the picture of a well-dressed man. What a difference after Burris!

Emily quickly sat in one of the leather chairs, with her back to the wall. She wanted to be aware of what was going on in the waiting room. Musgrove sat in one of the leather chairs facing her, but turned the chair slightly so he could also view the waiting room.

"Miss Smith ... may I call you Emily?"

"Yes, please do."

"We were called into this by the DEA, the Drug Enforcement Administration. Am I correct in assuming that you are in the employ of the DEA?"

"Actually we're funded by the Department of Agriculture; technically I'm employed by them as a botanist. Mr. Armitage, do you know who Mr. Armitage is ?"

"No."

"Mr. Armitage is our contact in Washington; in case of any emergency we were instructed to contact him."

"And you did that?"

"Yes, and he told me not to discuss anything with the local police but to cooperate fully with the FBI."

Musgrove gave a quiet grunt, presumably a grunt of satisfaction.

"Emily, usually, in an interrogation, which is what you and I are now engaged in, I would ask questions and you would answer. But this is not the same. I know you want to help us find the answers, in fact, you have a deep desire to find the answers. Instead of following the 'Q and A' routine, I just want you to start at the beginning, and tell me all that you know. If there's anything that isn't clear I'll interrupt you and ask for clarification, otherwise you just keep talking."

Already Emily felt kindly toward this man.

"A meeting was scheduled for eight o'clock this morning. I was late getting here; I had a flat tire and ended up taking a City bus. I had a little accident when I was alighting from the bus. I tore my stocking and messed up my skirt." Emily showed Musgrove the abrasion of her knee "I went right to the washroom and cleaned up, and then walked to the office."

"When I entered the office I noticed Mary Ann, our receptionist was not at her desk. I assumed she had been called into the meeting for some reason. I opened the door to the Board Room where the meeting was being held and found that all of them had been shot." Emily shuddered. Tears were clouding her vision.

"I panicked. I ran from the office and tried to take the elevator down. My only thought, I'm ashamed to say, was to escape from here. When the elevator door opened and I saw no one in there, my senses came back to me. I reentered the office, went to Mary Ann's desk and phoned Mr. Armitage. He said he would contact the FBI and I was to contact the local police. He told me not to give the police any information about our operation, but to cooperate fully with the FBI."

Musgrove interrupted, "I want to know what the meeting was about, but first, tell me who the victims were."

"I knew three of the victims. Mr. Andrews, Robert Andrews, was in charge, and Mary Ann was our secretary and receptionist. Alex Candejar was a biologist."

"Candejar started up our operation in Mexico. The other two men were from Colombia. I don't know anything about them."

Emily searched Musgrove's eyes; he said he would not interrupt unless he needed clarification, he looked at her with intently but said nothing.

"This is all very complicated," Emily continued. "I'd better explain first what our operation was all about or you'll never make any sense out of it."

She paused, took a deep breath and continued. "We were in the process of developing plant pathogens, targeted specifically at infecting and destroying the coca plant which is the precursor to cocaine. You may know that the US Government has spent many millions in South America to destroy coca fields, particularly in Colombia, but with only limited success."

"I assume you are referring to the use of crop-duster airplanes and the use of herbicides?"

"Yes, when using herbicides it's necessary to expose each plant in order to destroy a field of coca plants. If you had a field of, say, ten thousand plants, the crop duster would have to spray in strips, back and forth until the whole field had been covered. This is expensive as well as dangerous because it exposes the crop duster to rifle or machine gun fire from the ground."

"Using plant pathogens, if you infect just one plant in the ten thousand you still have the potential to destroy the whole field as the pathogen will spread from one plant to the next. Within one or two weeks, under ideal weather conditions, the entire field could be wiped out. And if the plant infection spreads from one field to the next, and then to the next, you would soon have an epidemic, spreading through the whole country."

Emily continued: "We started a small growing operation in Los Angeles County in the mountains northeast of here, three years ago. It was at a remote area, miles from anywhere at the end of a dirt road; complete isolation. There were three of us. We referred to the operation as the 'Farm'. This was strictly a clandestine operation. It was disguised as an ongoing botany study."

"It must have been lonely," Musgrove observed.

"It was but it had its compensations. For one thing the salary was good; I was making much more that I could have anywhere else. More important was that I was working very closely with two gifted scientists. Mr. Andrews held a doctorate in plant pathology - despite his doctorate he didn't use a title - we just addressed him as Mr. Andrews."

"Candejar was about forty. He had spent his entire career in biological research. I was just out of college and it was inspiring to be able to work with two such gifted men."

"Another perk was that we were allowed to take off one week in four; three weeks on and one week off. That's the equivalent of thirteen weeks vacation each year. But being so shut up and so isolated while at work, that was the only way we could keep our sanity. The only drawback was that in my free time I was able to prowl around the shopping malls, and that was hard on my bank account."

In response to her own wry remarks Emily smiled. She had a slightly wide mouth, perfect white teeth, and when she smiled her smile had startling effect on the observer. Musgrove gave and appreciative blink but immediately Emily felt guilty smiling at this time of tragedy.

"What did you do about security," Musgrove asked?

"We relied mostly on our remote location and the sign at the front gate. The property was surrounded by a chain link fence and there was a heavy chain and padlock on the gate; the sign said -

'NO TRESPASSING'
'US GOVERNMENT PROPERTY'

"Did anyone ever try to enter the property?"

"Two men drove up in a truck one day. They got out of the truck, looked at our building and examined the padlock. The building was as nondescript as a building could be; the front of the building was just a flat, white wall made of plywood panels, with a door in the middle and a window on each side. It was prefabricated and erected on the site in twenty-four hours."

"The men hung around for a couple of minutes and then got into their truck and left. I guess they were just curious."

"If they had attempted to enter the property what would have been your procedure?" Musgrove asked.

"There was a small three foot mast on the ridge of the roof. It had a red light on top. The light had a flasher. If anyone persisted the plan was that we would turn on the flasher. It wasn't connected to anything, but might scare them off. You'd call it a red herring I suppose."

Musgrove persisted, "And if that did not deter them?"

“We had a rifle and a shotgun. If they persisted we would fire a shotgun blast into the air from one of the side windows where we could not be observed: that would probably drive them off. You know what an enormously loud boom a shotgun makes.”

“And if it didn’t drive them off?”

“Then we would have to confront them directly. We would have the advantage of being behind building walls while they were out in the open.”

“Were you given instruction on the use of firearms,” Musgrove asked?

“Just the basics - load, aim, fire.”

“And if necessary,” Musgrove persisted, “would you have shot an intruder?”

Emily paused and reflected, she looked at Musgrove and said, “I don’t know.”

"One day I asked Candy," she stopped to explain. "Mr. Candejar, from day one, was always called 'Candy,' but Mr. Andrews, of course, was always called 'Mr. Andrews.’

Emily continued, "One day I asked Candy why the shot gun cartridge was so much larger than the rifle cartridge, maybe ten times as large. He took a shotgun cartridge, pried open the crimped front end and poured out the contents, numerous steel pellets, like the BB 's used in a BB gun.”

"These pellets," he said, "are about five times as heavy as the single bullet of a rifle. So they need five times as much explosive power to propel them. When you fire a shotgun the pellets scatter over a wide area; they were designed to shoot game birds forty or fifty yards away. But if you fired a shot at a man ten or twelve feet away, because of the enormous explosive charge, it would probably cut a bloody round hole in him, from front to back."

"So, if I had to do it, Mr. Musgrove? I don't know."

"Please continue, Emily," Musgrove said.

"We were eventually successful in producing a potent pathogen; we referred to it as the 'product'. In the meantime environmentalists started poking around. They always assume the worst and, even though they would have had no evidence of wrongdoing on our part, it was felt that they might stir up the media. We couldn't risk any exposure; it would only benefit the drug dealers if they knew what our objectives were."

"It was decided about six months ago to close down the operation and set up elsewhere; Candejar was sent to Puerto Vallarta in Mexico to set up there, and we moved to Los Angeles to open an office here."

"Why would you need an office in this city if you were no longer engaged in a farming operation?" Musgrove asked.

"When it was decided that we would close here, it was decided, as I said, that a new operation would be started up in Mexico. Our office here in Los Angeles was to handle the transition, and afterward to act as liaison between the various people connected with the operation."

"Only two of us at the farm came to Los Angeles, Mr. Andrews and myself . Mary Ann and Petula Clarkeson were hired when we opened the office here. That was about six months ago. Mary Ann was receptionist and Petula, we called her 'Petie,' was my assistant. Petie has the flu and hasn't been at work. That's why she wasn't at the meeting. And as I mentioned, Candejar went to Mexico to set up there."

"The product which we had produced at the farm was divided into two lots; one was brought here and the other, a smaller lot, was sent to Mexico so production could be continued there."

Musgrove scratched his head. "I'm a little, ...well not confused, but I'm wondering . . . the operation you describe, if successful, could totally destroy the cocaine industry in Colombia. Why would such a potentially devastating blow to the drug industry be in the hands of such a . . . please excusing me for putting it in these words Emily, such a 'Mickey Mouse' operation?"

"I guess they thought we couldn't pull it off. We still don't know if the plan we devised for the dissemination of the pathogen will work. Developing the pathogen was straightforward work; it took time but there was no doubt in our minds that we could create an effective product. But just like the dropping of the atomic bomb on Hiroshima, there was no way to determine what the results would be without actually doing it."

As an afterthought she added, "It was never stated but tacitly understood that if we were found out, Washington would deny any knowledge of our operation."

Emily continued. "We developed computer models and set up a comprehensive procedure. Everything was in place and that was the purpose of the meeting. Two of the men at the meeting were from Colombia. They were to take one of the lots of pathogen back to Colombia together with detailed written instructions on how the product was to be reproduced and then disseminated. That's where I came in. From the computer models I created the written documentation on dissemination. That is what I refer to as my 'notes."

Musgrove asked, "Who were the two Colombians?"

"I didn't know them by name. They were seated to the left of Mr. Andrews. Candejar from our Mexico operation was to his right. And Mary Ann . . . poor Mary Ann was lying face down on the floor. She was our receptionist and had no reason to be at the meeting; they must had called her in for some reason."

"Or the killer may have forced her in." Musgrove surmised. "All of the offices were ransacked; do you know what might have been taken?"

"Just the product. I had taken my notes home with me so I could review them once more before making a presentation to the Colombians at the meeting. The notes consisted of forty typewritten pages of data. That's why they ransacked the offices; the notes are just as important as the product itself. Computer disks with complete details of the program were in the safe in Mr. Andrews' office, but the safe wasn't touched, or at least if they did try to open the safe they weren't successful. In any event the disks were password protected so they wouldn't have been of any use to the killer."

"What exactly are the notes and why are they so important?" Musgrove asked.

"The notes are an abbreviated summary of how the pathogen was to be applied in the field. Having the product without the notes would be like giving a painter a gallon of paint without a brush. He'd have no way of using the paint. Without the notes, no one would know how to effectively distribute the pathogen. Using computer models we were able to develop a complete program relating to prevailing winds, ambient temperature moisture conditions and other variables"

"Yes, I have a pretty good picture of your operation. . . Let's get back to what happened this morning. Did you see anyone or anything unusual?"

"As I walked down the hallway to the office a man was approaching me. He wore a black fedora hat, the kind I've seen in the old black and white movies, with the brim turned down at the back as well as the front. I think they called it a 'slouch' hat. He was medium height and wore a brown jacket with a shirt unbuttoned at the neck. He had high cheekbones and sallow skin, very tight skin, as though it had been stretched over his face. He had a black pencil mustache. He wore sunglasses so I couldn't see his eyes."

"It looked as though he was heading for the stairway but when he was opposite the elevator, the door opened and a woman walked out. He made an abrupt ninety-degree turn into the elevator, and the elevator door closed. It was then that I went into the office and found that they had all been shot."

"Do you think he might have been the killer?" Emily asked.

"It's quite possible," Musgrove said.

Emily's eyes widened, "If I hadn't fallen when I got off the bus I would have gone right into the meeting instead of going to the washroom to clean up. If he was the killer I would have entered the office while he was still there. I would have ended up with a bullet hole in my head."

Emily was excited. "And come to think of it, if my car hadn't had a flat tire I would have been here before eight, and I would have been at the meeting and I would have ended up like the rest of them."

"Calm down Emily . . . there is more that I need to ask you. Did anyone know about the meeting, other than the persons who attended?"

Emily said, "No." But then she paused and added, "Except the man I had dinner with last night."

"And who was that?"

"His name is Mark Sheldon, I met him three weeks ago, at the market. It was Friday night and I had stopped to pick up something for dinner. I decided on a frozen dinner. His shopping cart crashed into mine."

Emily recalled the incident.

He said, "I'm sorry, I wasn't looking where I was going."

He was handsome, tall, with black wavy hair and brown eyes. He had exceptionally fine features, perfect nose, perfect mouth, the shape of his face. So perfect he looked almost effeminate, but he had a slightly projecting jaw; it gave him a rugged look and restored his masculinity.

"That's all right," Emily replied.

"I guess you're shopping for dinner tonight, the same as I am. I hate cooking for one, but I like it even less if I have to eat dinner alone in a restaurant."

Emily said, "I know what you mean."

"My name is Mark. I know we've just met, but perhaps we could have dinner together, instead of each of us eating alone?"

Emily was about to decline when he flashed a smile, perfect white teeth to match his other perfect features.

And he added, "Just dinner, no messing around."

Emily paused . . . and then thought, "What the hell. It's better than eating alone on a Friday night."

"I'll put this macaroni and cheese back in the freezer. If you like Italian there's a little Italian restaurant about three blocks from here."

"We drove separately, ate spaghetti, exchanged phone numbers and said good night."

"And you saw him again since then?" Musgrove inquired.

"We had dinner again last week. He said he was a sales representative for a computer software company, working out of San Francisco. He traveled a lot, but mostly in California. When I asked him anything about his personal life he seemed uncomfortable, almost evasive; I wondered if maybe he was married. And, of course, he may have wondered about me. When he asked me about my work I guess I was kind of evasive. I mean, if someone asks you about your work, and you like your work, which I do, you're more likely to blab on than to clam up. I guess I was giving him mostly 'yes' and 'no' answers."

"So our conversation reverted back to things like current weather conditions, the recent spike in gasoline prices, how much we were being screwed by the IRS, et cetera."

"What you're saying is that it wasn't too romantic," Musgrove surmised. "But you did see him again?"

"Yes, last night. We had dinner." Emily blushed slightly. "I was going to ask him about his marital status but then I lost my nerve."

“He said he had completed a big deal and wanted to celebrate. I assumed by ‘big deal’ he meant a big sale.”

“After dinner we went dancing. It was getting late and I told Mark I had to get home. We were having a good time and he pressed me to stay later. That's when I told him I had an important meeting at eight a.m. next morning and I wanted to get a decent night's sleep.”

He said, "That's pretty early for a meeting."

"I don't know why I said it, to justify my own position I suppose; I told him two of the men who would be attending the meeting had to catch an early flight and the meeting was scheduled to accommodate them."

Emily added, "I guess that wasn't very smart?" The thought reeled through Emily's mind, “Was Mark Sheldon part of this murderous episode? Had she betrayed the trust that Mr. Andrews had in her because of her loose tongue? And had she inadvertently sent Andrews and Mary Ann and Candejar and the others to their deaths?"

The color drained from Emily's face, it was as pale as the white wall behind her. Musgrove noticed her distress.

"I wouldn't jump to any conclusions, Emily. We know very little about this case so far."

"I'd like to look in the safe. Do you have the combination?"

"Yes I do."

It was a wall safe in Mr. Andrews' office. Emily worked the combination and opened the safe door. Inside were six floppy disks and a white envelope. Emily removed the disks and handed the envelope to Musgrove. There was money inside. He counted twenty twenties and a fifty.

"Four hundred and fifty dollars. Did he ever keep large sums of money in the safe?"

"Not to my knowledge. Everything was paid for by check."

"But you did see the envelope in the safe?"

"Yes," Emily replied, "but I had no reason to look into it, so I didn't. Does it matter?"

"If he kept large sums of money in the safe it might be a motive for robbery - we have to consider all of the possibilities."

"All right Emily, I may want to talk to you again. Do we have your phone number?"

"Yes." Emily stammered, "You . . . you do, I gave it to one of the officers."

Musgrove rose and went back to the crime scene.

As Emily watched Agent Musgrove leave she realized that the outer office was filled with people she didn't know. Some uniformed and some not. Some stood around the office, some passed back and forth into the various offices and then back into outer office.

Detective Johnson had been hanging around. When he saw that Musgrove had left he approached.

With an engaging smile he said, "Miss Smith, you said you had arrived here by bus. Could I offer you a ride home?"

To which Emily replied, "Yes, thank you. I'd appreciate that.

An officer on duty saw them into the elevator.

III

When the elevator door opened on the main floor there stood another police officer. There were two officers on the street keeping at bay a crowd of news reporters and cameramen.

Emily and Johnson crossed the wooden walkway and the officers stepped aside for them to pass.

Johnson said quietly to Emily, “Just walk straight ahead, as though no one else was near. Don’t turn your head. And don’t answer any questions.”

Reporters and cameramen crowded around. Johnson said, "Let us through please," as he pushed through the crowd, holding Emily by the arm.

And there was a barrage of questions. "Are you a witness to the murders?" "Who was the killer?" "How many people were killed?" Emily made no response. Eventually, concluding the two had nothing to offer, they lost interest.

Johnson pushed ahead still grasping Emily's arm and repeating himself several times, "Let us through please."

No wonder there was such a commotion. On the street there were dozens of police cars, ambulances and other vehicles. Traffic on the street was jammed, police officers were waving their arms, blowing their whistles, and directing angry motorists to alternate routes.

Johnson's car was parked on the street in front of the office building. He opened the front passenger door for her, and after she had settled in her seat, closed it with a smile. Emily was impressed. As attentive as he was, Mark Sheldon overlooked this simple courtesy.

When Johnson climbed into the car she said, "Thank you. I don't know what I would have done if I had been alone."

Johnson started up, and with the help of one of the traffic-directing cops, moved out onto the street, made a U-turn and headed west on Wilshire.

"You know where I live?" Emily asked.

"Your address was on the report you gave to the police officers who first attended."

Johnson continued, "I'm curious to know why the FBI jumped into this case."

"Then it would be best if you asked the FBI," was Emily's answer.

Johnson looked a little crushed; there was a tone of finality in Emily's reply and he knew he would get no further information from her.

"There's something *I'm* curious about," Emily said. "Why was Sergeant Burris pushing me so hard, and where did he go? I mean, he just seemed to vanish."

Johnson gave a muffled grunt. "To you Emily, this is probably the most horrendous day in your life. Most people never see even one dead person in their lives, except maybe in a funeral casket. You've seen five violent deaths, and three of them close associates."

"To the Police Department this is just a murder case. But to Sergeant Burris this is not just another murder case, but possibly the most important case of his career. Murders usually happen in ones and twos, but five murders! It rarely happens. And the Sergeant knew he was in one of the biggest cases in the history of the Los Angeles Police Department. Then, along comes the FBI and steals it away from him."

"Does that mean that the Los Angeles Police Department won't be investigating this any further?" she asked.

"No it doesn't, but if the case is solved most of the credit will go to the FBI. Burris will be mentioned only as an *also ran*."

"Turn left at the next corner," Emily instructed, "and three blocks down."

They were on a tree-lined street. Three blocks down Johnson made a U-turn to park in front of Emily's apartment building.

Emily said, "Thank you," and then added, "I haven't had a cup of coffee since I left here this morning. Would you like to come up for coffee?"

Johnson said with a grin, "Have you ever met a cop who turned down a cup of coffee?"

With policeman's curiosity Johnson stopped to look at the security system at the front entry.

"It operates through the telephone system. If someone buzzes my apartment my telephone rings. If he identifies himself to my satisfaction I buzz him in."

Johnson followed Emily into her third-floor apartment. It opened into a large living room, tastefully furnished with an upholstered sofa and arm chair, gray in color with a neat pattern; tables were glass-topped and modern framed prints decorated the walls. There was a small upholstered side chair and, by the entry, a small wooden table with a rectangular top and a single drawer. The lady at the antique store called it a 'telephone table' but the drawer wasn't large enough to hold a Los Angeles telephone directory; it was used for small items, pens, pencils, and writing pads. Emily kept her address book there.

"Very nice, Emily."

"Thank you. Until recently I worked out of the city and only lived here part time. But since I've been in the city permanently I appreciate it more."

A sliding glass door led to a balcony.

"Do you have a view?"

"I have a view of the other apartment buildings on the street, and there are lots of beautiful trees. Come and have a look."

Emily slid open the door and they walked out onto the balcony. Looking down from the third floor they saw the canopy of trees below, and neatly manicured lawns of the other buildings.

"I don't use it much," Emily said as they returned to the living room, "but it seems to add a feeling of spaciousness to the living room."

"It's very nice, Emily, I wish I had the same arrangement myself."

"Have a seat and I'll put the coffee on."

Reaching for the coffee Emily noticed one of the cupboard doors had been left ajar and closed it. One thing that she never did was to leave a cupboard door only partly closed. It always looked so untidy that way. She must have really been in a hurry this morning.

With the coffee set to brew she went to her bedroom to change. She removed her jacket and skirt and looked ruefully at her torn stocking and damaged black shoe, with the right heel bent out of shape. Maybe she could have the shoe repaired.

She slid the wardrobe door open to reach for a hanger. There were gaps here and there between groups of clothing. Strange, she didn't remember messing things up like that.

Emily changed into slacks and a sweater and returned to the kitchen. The brewing cycle was just completing. She poured two mugs of coffee, placed them on a tray with cream and sugar and returned to the living room.

"Cream and sugar, Detective?"

Johnson accepted and said, very seriously, "Call me Kevin, that's my first name, and if it's all right, I'll call you Emily."

"Of course, I'd like that," and she added, "You seem to be young to be a detective."

"I'm twenty-eight, and you're right. I *am* young to be a detective. I made a couple of lucky busts and got a citation. They gave me a shot at 'detective,' probably for public relations reasons and, of course, I grabbed the opportunity.

Johnson wasn't beautiful, or even handsome, Emily thought, but he was nice looking; and he had a way expressing his thoughts quietly and sincerely. He went on.

"I've only been with Detective Burris for three months. He resented me at first because of my limited experience, but I think he realized that I was trying hard and doing the best I could and he eased off on me. He's taught me a lot."

Emily went to the small table by the front door. She needed the number of the auto club so she could phone about her flat tire. Her address book was in the drawer of the telephone table. As she opened the drawer she noticed it had not been fully closed. It was a little sticky and it took and effort to close it fully. But Emily would not have left it an unclosed position.

"Someone has been in my apartment."

Johnson's eyebrows raised. "What do you mean?"

“In the kitchen I noticed that one of the cupboard doors had not been fully closed. And in my bedroom the clothes in the wardrobe had been messed up a bit. And now this," she pointed to the drawer. “I like everything to be in its place and I never would have left any of these things as I found them. I suppose from doing research I'm in the habit of making sure that everything fits into its proper place."

"Did you check all of the rooms?"

"All but the bathroom."

"Let's check." Johnson instinctively reached for his gun but left it in its holster. With Emily following he checked the bathroom, the kitchen, the bedroom and carefully looked through the wardrobe.

"Did you notice if anything else had been disturbed?"

"No, just the things I mentioned."

“And nothing has been taken?”

“As far as I can tell everything is still here.”

Johnson went to the entry door, examined the lock and door jamb. He checked the sliding glass door in the living room, went out onto the balcony and looked down at the street.

"No sign of a forced entry. Either the perpetrator had a key or picked the lock."

"Only the building manager has a key, but he wouldn't enter without permission."

"Let's talk to him anyway. He might have seen something,"

"Just a minute, I want to get the phone number of the auto club. I have to get my tire changed."

Kevin interrupted, "I've changed a lot of tires. Before you call the auto club let me look at it."

They stopped first at the manager's apartment. The manager, Reardon, answered the door but he didn't invite them in . . . No, he didn't enter Emily's apartment. He wouldn't do so without permission, except in an emergency. And no, he hadn't seen anyone in the hallways.

"What's all this fuss about a flat tire?" he asked.

Johnson said, "You know about the flat tire?"

"Sure, another detective was here this morning and I took him down to the garage."

Johnson looked at Emily and Emily looked at Johnson and they said in unison, "Burris!"

The elevator door opened onto the parking level. Emily walked to the left with Johnson following.

"This is my beautiful silver Mercedez," she said as they approached her automobile.

Johnson whistled. "Very nice," he said.

"It cost more that I could afford, but I love it."

"You're confusing my thinking, Emily. Men usually spend more on cars than they should and women spend more on clothes that they don't need. You seem to have reversed the procedure."

"Unfortunately Kevin, I also spend more on clothes that I don't need. So now I'm turning into a budget freak."

Kevin looked at the flat tire with a pretended grimace, opened the trunk, removed the spare tire, and the tire iron and jack, and rolled the spare to the right rear. He looked down and said, "Emily, you didn't have a flat tire. Your car has been sabotaged."

When Emily came closer he said, "Look, the valve stem has been cut off.""

"Does that mean that the tire is ruined?"

"Just the opposite. All they have to do is remove the tire and insert a new valve stem. How long has your car been parked here?"

"Since yesterday. I came home from work about six."

"Were you home all evening?"

"No, my date picked me up. I met him at the front door. I got back home before midnight."

Johnson jacked up the rear of the car. "I'd say whoever sabotaged your tire didn't want you to get to the meeting this morning on time. Any idea who that might be?"

The thought flashed through Emily's mind, "Mark Sheldon." He had been acting a little strange last night. When they arrived back at Emily's apartment he parked his car on the street in front. At the entry to the building Emily was about to say 'Good Night' when Sheldon said, "I'll see you to your door."

At the door Emily turned and said, "Thanks Mark, I had a really nice time."

"I could use some coffee."

"Sorry Mark, I have to be up early so I'll have to say goodnight."

He gave her a perfunctory kiss and said, "Good night."

As Emily entered her apartment Sheldon was waiting for the elevator. "Not a very passionate kiss," she thought, "maybe he was just a little upset because didn't invite him in." She really liked Mark and thought he felt the same about her.

Emily looked down at Detective Johnson. "My date, Mark Sheldon saw me to my door last night. He could have entered the garage before he left."

"Any reason why he should?"

"None that I can think of."

"Will you be all right in your apartment tonight?"

"Yes, there's a dead bolt which operates only from the inside, and also a heavy chain."

Johnson finished installing the spare tire. "I'll file a report on your suspected burglary, but there isn't much to go on. No sign of forced entry, and apparently nothing stolen. I don’t think it will create a lot of excitement."

He handed Emily his card. "If you need anything call me. I jotted down my home phone number on the back."

"Thank you Kevin, let me write down my phone number for you in case you want to get in touch with me."

She took out a small pad, wrote down her number.

"No business card?"

"For security reasons we didn't use them."

Kevin rode with Emily out to the street.

"Don't forget to call me if you need anything, Emily."

"I won't Kevin, and thanks again for your help."

Emily pondered the situation in her apartment. Was she just imagining that things were out of place? She had slept late and was almost in a panic about being late for the meeting. Maybe she did leave the cupboard door open. But her closet, she would have had no reason to move any of the clothes around. She went over it again in her mind. She removed her black suit. Her black shoes were on the shoe rack on the floor, so she didn't have to disturb anything looking for them.

As far as the telephone table was concerned, she had no reason to open the drawer; she probably hadn't looked in the drawer for a week or more. The more she thought about it the more she was firm in her conclusion that someone had been in the apartment.

IV

When her tire had been replaced Emily checked her cell phone. Petie had called four times. Emily didn't want to talk to her on the telephone. Petie was too excitable and it could only have been a garbled conversation at best. But now, with her personal business done, Emily headed for Petie's apartment.

When Emily rang her bell, through the door Petie's soft voice inquired, "Who is it?"

"It's me. Emily."

The door burst open. Petie threw her arms around Emily.

"Oh Emily, I've been so frightened. I phoned you over and over but you didn't answer.I thought the detective might have made a mistake. He told me you were O.K."

"There was a detective here?"

"Sergeant Burris, he said all of the people at the meeting had been killed, except you."

"What else did he ask about?"

"He seemed to be more interested in my health than anything else. He wanted to know when I took sick. I told him I had come home early from work on Wednesday and I hadn't been out of here since."

"I guess he just wanted to find out if you may have intentionally avoided the meeting," Emily surmised.

"What's it all about Emily? I know my job was just to assist you with statistical analysis, but considering all that's happened I think someone owes me an explanation, and you're the only someone I know. Am I in danger of being murdered?"

Emily paused. Petie was right. She did deserve an explanation. But what to tell her, and how much?

"No you're not in danger of being murdered, Petie. You were kept in the dark about our operation because the fewer who knew what was going on the less chance there was that someone might slip out with something." Emily bit her tongue. The thought plagued her, "Had she inadvertently given information about the meeting to Mark, that resulted in the death of so many?"

Petie looked puzzled; Emily added, "You were hired to assist me with statistical work and you did it admirably well."

Petie cocked her pretty head, rolled her blue eyes and gave a pleasant smirk of approval.

Emily continued, "You majored in biology, so you were familiar with most of the technical language we would be using. You were a straight 'A' student so we knew we could count on you for efficiency and insight. You were aware that we were investigating plant pathogens."

Petie nodded and Emily continued.

"What you weren't told was that we planned to infect the coca fields in Colombia with the pathogen. Colombia produces about eighty per cent of all of the world's cocaine; cocaine is made from the coca plant."

"The United States has spent many millions helping Colombia combat the drug trade. In the growing fields they have used herbicides, but that has been costly and not too effective. At the time you were hired we had already produced plant pathogens that could devastate a coca plantation. But now, simply put, it was a matter of delivery; how do we introduce the pathogen to the coca plant?"

Petie gave an expectant nod.

"That's where you and I came in. The computer models we used examined weather conditions, temperatures, moisture and rain, prevailing winds, and, of course, many other factors. It then spit out its conclusions; I put these into a condensed typewritten summary that could be understood by whoever was assigned the task of applying the pathogen to the coca fields. I referred to the summary as my "notes."

Petie asked, "And the meeting was to set this in motion?"

"Yes, the Colombians were to return to their home base at Bogota with the pathogen and set up operations much the same as we had established here. They had separate instructions on how to reproduce the pathogen so they would have a continual supply as it was needed. And, of course, they would carry out the dissemination of the pathogen into the coca fields."

Petie asked, "How do you think the killer knew about the meeting? I mean he would have to have known the exact time it was scheduled; or was it just coincidence that he got there when the meeting started?"

With a pang that shot through her heart Emily said, "There may have been a leak."

Petie had an exuberant personality. Everything she did, she did with enthusiasm and bubbling grace. Most people didn't take her seriously. Petite, five foot three, blue eyes, and lustrous black hair; with her effervescence Petie still gave the impression of being a teenager. She was twenty-five.

But Emily had observed how diligently she had attacked her work, and how much insight she had in helping to evaluate the mountains of data that had to be processed. And now she had come up with another astute insight. 'How did the killer know not only the date, but the exact time that the meeting was to be held?'

"What I'm wondering now," Petie said, "with Mr. Andrews and Mary Ann gone, do we go back to work on Monday or do we join the ranks of the unemployed?"

"I don't know, Petie. Mr. Armitage will be calling me from Washington, probably tomorrow, and I'm sure he will have it sorted out by then."

"Who is Mr. Armitage?"

"He's located in Washington. He was in charge of the operation. I was given his phone number to call in the case of emergency. I phoned him this morning and told him what had happened. He said he would be in touch."

"Anyway Petie, I'm getting hungry. Do you have anything to eat?"

"Not much, payday is on Monday, and besides, I haven't been out of here for three days."

Emily took stock of the contents of the refrigerator in five seconds. Eggs, yogurt, and a carton of orange juice.

She returned to the living room. "Which do you prefer, Chinese or pizza?" Petie opted for pizza.

Twenty minutes later the door chime sounded. Emily put her ear to the door and asked, "Who is it?"

"Pizza delivery."

"Just a minute." She turned and said quietly to Petie, "See if his car is outside."

Petie ran to the window and nodded, "yes." Emily opened the door and accepted the pizza.

When the pizza man had left Petie asked, "Do we have to be that careful?"

Emily replied."Yes Petie, we do." And she added, “Just a precaution.” But Emily wasn’t as confident of their safety as her words conveyed.

V

Emily returned home about eight and then realized she wasn't as brave as she thought she was in the morning when Detective Johnson was there. She checked the dead bolt and chain on the entry door twice. She looked down from her third floor balcony.

"No one could climb up that far from ground level," she thought. Still, to make sure she removed the handle from her mop and placed it to block any movement of the sliding glass door leading from the balcony to the living room.

She tried to read but couldn't concentrate. She turned on television but, flipping channels, couldn't find anything that held her attention. She decided to go to bed; she was tired but felt too keyed up to sleep; maybe she could read in bed for a while.

In bed Emily made a concerted effort to relax. She put down her book. "Close your eyes," she told herself, "let all of the energy drain out of your body. Relax, relax."

She felt the tension draining from her body; maybe she would be able to fall asleep after all.

Then the telephone rang. She looked at her alarm clock. Just after ten. "Who could be calling at this late hour?"

"Hello?"

"It's me, Mark. I'm downstairs, please let me in."

He sounded distressed. Emily hit the number nine button on the phone and this activated the lock mechanism of the main entry door, with an accompanying buzz. She ran to the entry door of her apartment. Now she wondered if she should let him in. If he had anything to do with the massacre at the office she could be in grave danger. But surely he wouldn't take a chance on being seen if he intended to do her harm. She decided to let him in.

Two minutes later there was an uneven knocking on the door. Emily turned the dead bolt, removed the chain and turned the door knob. The door swung inward; Emily stepped back and Mark Sheldon pitched forward onto the floor. There was a bullet hole in the back of his jacket, surrounded by a circle of blood.

He raised himself onto his hands and knees.

Emily cried out, "Mark, Mark, who did this to you?"

Sheldon mumbled, "Wan . .. wan .. . duh," and then fell forward onto his face. Emily was afraid to touch him. It looked like he was dead.

This was not 'deja vu,' it was real. The same thing had happened this morning, only hours earlier.

She picked up the telephone and dialed nine-one-one. When the operator answered she said, "A man has been shot."

Then she phoned Kevin Johnson. When he answered she said, "Kevin, Mark Sheldon came to my apartment, someone shot him. I think he's dead."

"Who is Mark Sheldon?"

"He's a man I had dinner with last night."

"I'll be right over."

“Please hurry Kevin. I’m afraid, and I feel like running from here and never coming back.”

Johnson arrived five minutes after the police officers. Emily was in the bedroom. She gave him a weak smile and said, "I couldn't stand it in there. Is he really dead?"

"Yes he is Emily. Tell me what happened."

"I went to bed at ten o'clock. The phone rang. It was Mark. He said he was downstairs. I let him in. When I opened the door he fell forward onto his face."

"Did he say anything?"

"He raised himself onto his hands and knees. I asked him who shot him and he said . . . I thought he said, 'Wanda.' Then he collapsed."

"Who is Wanda?"

"I have no idea."

"What was your relationship with Sheldon?"

"It wasn't a relationship," Emily replied. "I met him three weeks ago. We had dinner. Last night was the third time I had seen him. He was a computer software salesman. We got along very well together. I liked him very much."

"Did you know he was FBI?"

"FBI!" Emily was startled. "Do you mean he wasn't a computer software salesman? I wonder why Mr. Musgrove didn't know about that?"

"I don't know, but he was carrying an FBI ID."

Emily tried to sort out the confusing picture in her mind. If Mark was an FBI agent why was he posing as a computer software salesman? He didn't just bump into her at the market, he was there to pick her up when his shopping cart crashed into hers.

She remembered now that his cart had nothing in it. He wasn't shopping for his dinner as he said. She thought he had asked her to have dinner with him because he found her attractive. But now, with a twinge of wounded pride, she had to admit to herself that he had just 'picked her up' to suit his own purposes.

But what did this all mean? Why would an FBI agent want to become acquainted with her? And why didn't Mr. Musgrove know who Sheldon was? Musgrove was obviously in a high position in the FBI or he wouldn't have been called in. Presumably this was because of Armitage's influence in Washington. Was Musgrove just keeping her in the dark about Sheldon?

"Will Sergeant Burris be coming here tonight?"

Johnson said, "No, he likes to work from nine to five. I'll tell him about it in the morning. He'll chew me out for not calling him but I'll tell him I thought he needed his rest."

"Do you need me for anything else?"

"No but I don't think you should stay here tonight."

"I know." Emily picked up the phone and dialed Petie's number. When Petie's sleepy voice answered Emily said, "You're going to have an overnight guest." Before Petie could ask any questions Emily hung up.

To Kevin she said, "Would you mind coming to the garage with me?"

"Not at all."

"I'll just get a few things for overnight." She packed a few things in a bag and returned. They took the elevator down to the garage. Kevin rode with her in her car to the street. His own car was parked there.

"Kevin I really appreciate the help you've given me. I haven't been completely forthcoming with you. I was instructed to keep close mouthed."

"I understand Emily," Kevin said, and he looked at Emily intently. Emily was dead tired but in the back of her mind she thought she saw a little passion in his eyes.

Kevin said 'good night' and Emily drove on to Petie's.

VI

When Emily knocked on the door she heard Petie's quiet voice say, "Who is it?"

"It's Emily, Petie." Petie opened the door and Emily added, "I told you on the phone I was on my way over. Who else did you think it was at this time of night?"

"I'm sorry Emily, I'm nervous. Why did you come back here to stay with me? I mean, you're welcome, but did something happen at your apartment?"

“I’m sorry too, Petie, for snapping at you, but something terrible has happened and I’m upset. . You never met Mark Sheldon, Petie, but you remember that I told you I had been seeing him.”

Petie nodded.

“Well he came to my apartment tonight, just after ten. He had been shot.”

Petie, wide eyed asked, “Is he all right?”

“No, he’s dead. Someone shot him in the back”

Petie was visibly shaken. “Oh Emily, what does it all mean; first those terrible murders at the office, and now another one at your apartment?” She added, “I’m frightened.”

“We’ll be all right, Petie. No one knows we’re here.” Emily wished she felt as assured feeling her words were meant to convey. “Anyway, it’s after midnight and I’m dead tired.” She wished she hadn’t used the word 'dead'. "We'll talk about it in the morning. If you'll get me a blanket and a pillow I'll crash out here on the sofa."

Petie returned with the bedding. "I'd let you have my bed but it's full of germs."

Emily yawned and said, "That's OK."

* * *

In the morning Emily fried the eggs and heated the remainder of the pizza in the microwave. She plugged in the cord of coffee maker. It gave a hiss and a pop and smoke and sparks streamed from the end of the cord. She unplugged it and noticed the cord was frayed and the wires exposed.

"Where did you get this thing, Petie?"

"I bought it at a thrift store."

"It figures," Emily said.

"When I moved in here," Petie explained, "this was my first apartment and there were a lot of household things I didn't have. I had to cut corners so I bought several things second hand."

Emily took a knife, cut off the burned wiring, stripped the wires and refastened them. She plugged in the coffee maker.

While Emily served the breakfast Petie monitored the coffee maker.

"Nothing is happening," she reported.

"It must have tripped a breaker. Where's your electrical panel?"

"In the closet off the bedroom."

Emily returned from the bedroom, "It was the breaker, it should be working now."

"Yes," Petie said, "I can see it starting to warm up."

"We'll have coffee for dessert," Emily replied.

Breakfast of orange juice, eggs and warmed up pizza; Emily's stomach groaned its discontent.

"Emily," Petie asked, "how did you learn to this kind of thing, I mean, like fixing a broken coffee maker?"

"Before we opened the office in Los Angeles three of us worked in a lab in an isolated area in the in the mountains, Mr. Andrews and myself, and a biologist named Candejar. If something broke you didn't just pick up the telephone and call for a repair man. And for security reasons we couldn't have called a repair man anyway.

"Andrews and Candejar were scientists. They were totally incompetent when it came to anything else. So if anything broke, either I fixed it or it stayed broken. So I learned to fix things as I went along."

Petie gave Emily an admiring look. "Gee you're smart, Emily!"

Emily gave her an affectionate pat on the head.

"We did a lot of barbecuing and one day Candejar, we called him 'Candy,' decided he would barbecue some steaks. We had a gas barbecue and we used an igniter to start the gas burning. The igniter was a long rod with a flint and flywheel device at the end. At the other end was a pistol grip with a trigger. When you pulled the trigger it made a spark at the end. The idea was that you first turned on the gas and then pulled the trigger and the tiny spark set the gas on fire."

"Candy turned on the gas but he couldn't get a spark out of the starter. He went to the kitchen to get some matches but he forgot to turn off the gas. When he returned and struck a match, so much unburned gas had accumulated that, 'POOF!' a giant explosion."

"Candy got away with just singed eyebrows; I put the barbecue back together and rinsed off the steaks. When they were done they were delicious; and Candy gave up barbecuing forever."

"All this talk about food," Petie said, "is making me hungry."

"We'll have to go out and get some food or we'll both starve to death. But Armitage said he'd phone today so We'd better wait till he calls. It's past noon in Washington."

"Emily, it must have been lonely up there in the mountains?"

"Yes, it was Petie, just the three of us, in what was essentially isolation, but we had to maintain complete privacy. I did a lot of reading. Mr. Andrews had an extensive library."

"When we needed supplies one of us would leave at dawn, before anyone was up, and then wait till dawn the next day to return. We took turns so each of us would have a little break now and then. We did that for more than three years. When they decided to close down the operation I can't say that I was unhappy.'

"Why couldn't you do that after dark?"

"Cars have headlights, Petie. And headlights attract attention. And people who live in remote areas see anything that moves."

"Emily there's one thing I'm curious about."

"What's that?"

"That little cassette that the pathogen was contained in. How could that small amount be used to infect an entire field, let alone an entire country?"

"That was the part you weren't familiar with because I had just completed my notes. It was under the heading 'Propagation'. If you hadn't taken sick you would have reviewed it on Wednesday or Thursday."

Emily continued, "A quantity of coca leaves would be shredded and a small amount of pathogen would be added. This would be allowed to 'cook' for three to five days giving it a stir now and then, and by that time the pathogen would have reproduced exponentially, similar to making beer or wine using yeast. Yeast is a 'friendly' bacteria, but is a bacteria just the same as our pathogen."

"The shredded coca leaves would then be disseminated over the coca fields at an opportune time. Some of the brew would be saved and added to newly shredded leaves and the process would be repeated. This is the same method some bakers use to make bread. They set aside some of the dough they have made and use it for the next batch of bread. It's called a starter."

"The purpose of the cassette was to enable us to carry the pathogen from place to place in a convenient form. Naturally you couldn't carry a bucket of fermenting coca leaves from place to place. So we condensed the pathogen into dried form and put it into a cassette. It looks like tobacco but it's filled with nasty little microbes that love to infect coca plants. In dried form it will last almost indefinitely, especially if refrigerated."

Emily's cell phone rang, exactly ten a.m. She said, "Hello, this is Emily Smith."

"This is Armitage, I have things sorted out for you."

"Yes sir."

"First I should tell you that you are not in anyway obligated to undertake the task I'm going to describe to you. You were hired as a biologist and your job classification has not changed. However, with Andrews and Candejar, out of the picture we have no one with knowledge of this operation. I don't think there is any real danger, but I'm going to ask you to carry out something that is essential to the fulfillment of our program and it might involve some risk."

"Yes sir, and I assume you heard about Mark Sheldon?"

"Yes, that's a puzzle. He wasn't working for us so we're thinking that he must have been involved in some other investigation and just blundered into this. Anyway the FBI is looking into it."

Armitage continued, "You were not connected with or given details about the Mexico operation. It was set up as a clandestine operation and carried out by Candejar, near Puerto Vallarta, much the same as you had carried out in California. It did not have the approval or even the knowledge of the Mexican government."

"Oh God," Emily thought, "he's going to ask me to continue the operation in the Mexican jungle." After the months of isolation in the California mountains, and then the comparative luxury of living in Los Angeles, she couldn't stand another period of exile.

"The operation in Mexico has not been a success. We had counted on the isolation of the laboratory to provide us with security, and that it did. However, on the negative side it made communication difficult, and in addition, all materials and supplies needed in the operation had to be carried in by hand, and this placed an unwonted burden on Candejar and his assistant."

"We are going to abandon Puerto Vallarta. What we now need you to do, Emily, is to pick up the product that Candejar had taken from Los Angeles to Mexico, and deliver it to the American Embassy in Bogota, Colombia. If we had the foresight we would have had Candejar close down before he came to Los Angeles, but he still had a small amount of work to do so we decided to have him carry on till he end of the month."

Emily gasped into the telephone and her tensed shoulders sagged in relief. And her mind said, "Is that all?"

Armitage heard Emily's gasp and inquired, "Emily, are you all right?"

"Oh . . . yes sir."

"I'll send you written instructions. And, according to the dossier I have here, there was a female employee named Clarkeson."

"Yes sir, as a matter of fact, she's right here with me. I'm staying with her in her apartment temporarily."

"Two young women are less conspicuous than one young woman traveling alone. Since you will want to avoid attracting attention it would be desirable for you to have a traveling companion. Ask Miss Clarkeson if she would be willing to travel with you, and if so, does she have a passport. I'm assuming that you have one."

With her hand over the phone Emily turned to Petie and said, "He wants us to pick up the product at Puerto

Vallarta and deliver it to Columbia. Are you OK with that?"

Petie nodded her head, "Yes."

"Do you have a passport?"

Petie shook her head, "No."

Emily spoke into the phone, "Mr. Armitage, Miss Clarkeson is willing to accompany me, but she doesn't have a passport."

"All right, have a passport photo taken and fax it to me with a copy of her driver's license. We have her personal data on file. You will have written instructions by Monday morning. Just one more thing, the computer disks recording your operations, do you have them?"

"Yes, everything was recorded on six floppy disks. I have them here with me. Also, it was arranged that I would give a presentation at the meeting, outlining the operation. This was to be for the benefit of the Colombians. I had compiled forty pages of typewritten notes and I have them with me."

"All right, fax all of that to me with the photos of Clarkeson. And send the floppy disks to me separately by courier service.

"Mr. Armitage?"

"Yes." He said it with a kind of finality, as though he had thought the conversation had already ended.

“I hate to bring this up at this time. But we all have payments to meet, rent, car payments and so forth,” Emily was thinking of her own car payment which was due next week.

She continued, “Payday is on Monday, and frankly Sir, with everything in such a mess and the office closed, we are in limbo as to our future income.”

“I’ll see that it’s taken care of.” He Hung up.

“Come on Petie, we’re going shopping.”

“What for?”

“First we're going to buy some clothes for our trip, then I’m going to buy a new pair of black shoes to replace the ones I damaged, then we’re going to buy some groceries, and then we’re going to have your picture taken.”

In the department store each of them bought a dress-up dress and some casual clothes. Emily bought a pair of black medium heels to replace the damaged ones.

They were about to leave when Emily spotted a pair of shoes on display. Not spikes but pretty high. They were beautiful and she had to have them. She would need a nice pair of shoes for the trip to Colombia, and besides, she hadn't bought anything for herself for at least two weeks. Seventy-five dollars! a budget buster, but what the heck, she might not be going on an important journey like this for a long time.

"I'll take these also," she told the sales clerk.

They stopped at a photo studio that displayed a sign which said, "Passport Photos."

While waiting for the photographer to set up Petie started clowning, making faces at the camera and generally acting up.

"All right Petie, settle down."

“I’m just letting off a little steam, Emily. I’ve been cooped up in my apartment for three days.”

Emily took out a comb and straightened Petie's lustrous black hair. She wore it short and straight and it enhanced her petite image. It framed her face and deepened the blueness of her eyes.

With the picture taking done the photographer made a copy of Petie's drivers' license. He also copied Emily's notes for her. Then to the express office where they sent the photos and the driver's license and the copied notes to the address that Emily had received from Armitage.

"OK Petie, that takes care of business. Let's have some lunch and then we'll buy some food for dinner."

VII

On Monday morning a small box arrived by courier. Emily signed for it and placed it on the dining room table.

"Quick Petie, get a knife."

Petie was excited. She ran to the kitchen and returned with a knife. Emily slit the tape sealing the box and opened it. Inside was a large, sealed envelope.

"Quick Petie, get some scissors." Petie ran to her desk and brought the scissors.

"This is just like Christmas," Petie cried.

Emily cut open the envelope and dumped the contents on the dining room table. There were four smaller envelopes inside. One was marked, 'Petula Clarkeson.' Petie opened the envelope with the scissors and inside found,

"My passport!"

"That was fast," Emily observed, "it took me three weeks to get mine."

"You just don't know the right people, Emily."

Emily cut open the largest of the three remaining envelopes and shook out the contents.

"Money!"

There were four packs of one-hundred-dollar bills. They counted, twenty-five hundred each, a total of ten thousand dollars.

Petie cried, "Ten thousand dollars. I've never seen so much money!"

The next envelope contained a letter; looking at the bottom of the letter Emily noted that it was signed by Mr. Armitage. It read:

"Enclosed are the following:

1) Passport of Petula Clarkeson

2) Ten thousand dollars in cash

3) A money belt

You are to carry out the following:

Proceed to Puerto Vallarta and check into the De Anza Hotel. You will have to arrange your own reservations.

Our representative will contact you there and give you proper identification

You will proceed with him to the laboratory site and pick up the product and any other data or information that may be of use

Returning to Vallarta you will arrange for flights to Mexico City and then on to Bogota. Check into the Simon Bolivar Hotel in Bogota and proceed as soon as possible to the United States Embassy. Further instructions will await you there

Any money, personal identification cards and such which are not needed immediately on each day of travel are to be kept in the money belt which is to be worn either by you or by Miss Clarkeson

We have not had time to make salary arrangements for you. In the meantime you are authorized to draw upon

> the funds enclosed herewith. It is suggested that your withdraws should not exceed the amounts which you would normally have received in your salary checks.
> All withdrawals will be deducted from future salary payments which have accrued to you.
> Keep receipts for all other expenses.
> I expect that the time element for this operation should not exceed four or perhaps five days.
> The combination for the safe at the Mexico location is given below. Candejar normally would have stored the product in the refrigerator in the laboratory but in view of his planned visit to Los Angeles it was placed in the safe. His only assistant, the gardener, is believed to be reliable but is youthful and it was not felt that anything so valuable should be entrusted to him.
> When you have reviewed the foregoing contact me by telephone for further instructions
>
> 2 L 20 - R 63 - 2 L 50

Emily looked at Petie, "He didn't waste any words trying to be polite."

Petie replied, "Anyone who can dispense this much cash doesn't have to be polite." And she added, "Let's look at the money belt."

Petie didn't wait for the scissors; with zestful enthusiasm she tore open the last envelope with her petite fingers and removed the contents.

The money belt was a doubled strip of nylon mesh about four inches wide. When Petie dangled it in front of Emily it looked to be about three feet long. There were several pockets built in to the strip. The pockets had waterproof seals. There were Velcro fasteners at each end of the belt.

Petie said, "You have the twenty-one inch waistline, Emily, so I think you should wear it."

"That's twenty-four inch, Petie, and thank you for the phony compliment."

Emily wrapped the belt around her waist. Even with the money added any change in the appearance of her waistline wouldn't be noticeable.

"I guess I had better call Mr. Armitage. Before I do Petie, are you sure you want to be involved in this?"

"Mary Ann was my friend, Emily. We went everywhere together and I'll miss her. If I can do anything to get even with these evil people I will." Petie was trembling and there were tears in her eyes.

Emily picked up her phone and dialed Armitage. When he answered she said, "This is Emily Smith."

"You have received the package and you understand the instructions?"

"Yes sir."

"There have been some changes. It has been decided that a laboratory will be set up within the grounds of the US Embassy in Bogota. You will be in charge of the setup operation. You are the only one who knows how to do this. Your computer disks will be forwarded to the Embassy together with password information and, I understand, they contain a complete record of your California operation. It will be a matter of duplicating the work which you did in California, but on a smaller scale. Smaller scale because the Embassy has limited space within their grounds."

"When you have checked into your hotel at Puerto Vallarta go to the hotel restaurant. You will be met there by Candejar's gardener, his name is Arturo Martinez."

"Martinez will take you to the farm which is about thirty-five miles from Puerto Vallarta. When you have picked up the product you will return to Puerto Vallarta and proceed on to Bogota. I have instructed Martinez to accompany you to Bogota as he has the experience you will need to set up a growing operation."

"We had not considered the contingency that would prevent Candejar from returning to Mexico. Otherwise we would have arranged to have the product stored at a more accessible location. Martinez is a young man, his dossier says twenty-one. It was not felt that he was mature enough to be entrusted with the security of the product, hence the necessity of having you pick it up. The combination of the safe in which the product is stored is at the bottom of the instruction sheet which the courier delivered to you."

The thought ran through Emily's mind, "Martinez is twenty-one, Petie is twenty-five, and at twenty-seven I'm the old lady in this group!"

"Mr. Armitage."

"Yes."

"Miss Clarkeson agreed to accompany me, on the understanding that we would be away from Los Angeles for only a brief period. Now, as you indicated, this has been much extended. I think we should know approximately what period of time we will be expected to remain in Bogota; and with that information I'll be able to find out from Miss Clarkeson if she accepts the new arrangement."

"Of course," Armitage replied, "I can't give you an exact time period. You will have your own assistant with you, Miss Clarkeson, and Martinez to handle the gardening. The Colombians will assign two experienced biologists, so you will have a staff of five, including yourself."

"You already have the pathogen and the formula for producing more. You would know this better than I, but I would think of this as more of a mechanical operation, one that should not take long to complete. Give yourself a week to settle in, thirty days to work out a program, and another two or three weeks to wind it up. That would be about eight or nine weeks, total. The Colombians should be able to take over by that time."

Emily was thinking, "I wish I could be as optimistic as you." She knew how things could go wrong, and wrong and wrong.

But she replied to Armitage, "All right, but I'll have to ask Miss Clarkeson if she agrees to the change. You will remember that the original arrangement was based on a time period of four or five days. I can ask her now if you would like to hold, or I can call you back."

"Ask her now and I'll hold."

Emily put the palm of her hand over the telephone and turned to Petie. "He wants us to set up an operation in Bogota, instead of being away four or five days we would be away eight or nine weeks, are you game?"

Petie put the palms of her hands over her eyes. She leaned forward and put her elbows on her knees. After a few moments she sat back, eyes uncovered and said, "I really don't want to, but I have to, for Mary Ann. I'll go."

"Mr. Armitage."

"Yes."

"Miss Clarkeson is agreeable to the change."

"All right, proceed as quickly as you can. You have never met Martinez. He will be given instructions to meet you in the hotel restaurant. He will ask if you are Emily Smith. When you acknowledge he will say, 'I'm sorry to hear that your mother is not well.' You will respond by saying, 'She is much better now, thank you.' He will then advise you of the arrangements he has made regarding your visit to the laboratory site."

Armitage continued, "Remember that you and Miss Clarkeson will no longer be biologists. You will be agents for the DEA working in foreign countries. In terms of the vernacular you are 'Spies'. You haven't had any training in this respect and under normal circumstances you would not be asked to undertake this task. My best advice to you is to play your role as tourists, and if you are being questioned about anything, do not volunteer any information that has not been asked for."

"Do you have any questions?"

"No sir."

"Then I wish you good luck." He hung up.

Emily turned to Petie. "We have been cleared for takeoff Petie, and guess what? We are no longer biologists, we are," she spelled it out, "S-P-I-E-S."

"Spies!" Petie gasped. Then she began to whirl around the room with her full exuberance, and began crying out, "I'm a spy, I'm a spy, I'm a spy!"

But then she stopped and came to Emily. She was crying, sobbing. "Oh Emily, I'm so frightened, with all of these murders, and all of these terrible people. Who will take care of us when were in Mexico, or Colombia?"

Emily put her arms around her and put her head on her shoulder. Petie was still sobbing.

"Never mind, little one. I'll look out for the two of us."

In that instant Emily's relationship with Petie changed from friend and business associate to mother and big sister.

Emily picked up the phone and called Kevin Johnson. When he answered she said, "This is Emily, you said I could call you."

"Sure Emily, I'm glad to hear from you."

"Could I ask a favor Kevin?"

"Ask away." he replied.

"I need to pick up some things at my apartment; I'm uneasy about going in there alone."

"Your apartment is still under police seal so you wouldn't be able to enter by yourself. Would you like me to pick you up?"

"That would be great, Kevin, if you don't mind.

"I'll be there in half an hour."

VIII

Kevin removed the yellow police tape from the apartment door. When they entered Emily noticed there were still blood stains on the carpet where Mark had collapsed.

"Did they find out anything about Mark, and why he was here?"

"I probably shouldn't tell you this," Kevin said, " but they found out that he was not an FBI agent. He was carrying a phony ID. His name was not Mark Sheldon; that was an alias. His real name was Michael Shannon. He served time in prison for embezzlement and fraud. He had also been charged with burglary but that was dropped when he pled guilty to the other charges. He *was* a computer software salesman; he took computer courses while he was in prison. And oh, yes . . he *was* married. His wife is currently serving time for grand theft, she was part of a gang that stole jewelry, expensive jewelry from jewelry stores."

Emily was dumbfounded! "How could such a nice, handsome, personable man be such a scoundrel?"

The gnawing thought came back to Emily, "She had told him the date and time of the meeting. Had he used that information to set up the murderous event at the office?"

She asked Kevin, "Do you think he had anything to do with the massacre at the office?"

"Not likely; con men, that's what he was, a con man. Con men usually don't resort to violence. They prefer to stick the knife in another way. They gain your trust by using personality and charm. They're not interested in hurting you, just separating you from your bank account."

"He may have extracted information about the meeting from you, and passed it on to the killer, but it isn't likely that he had anything more than that to do with it. My guess is that he was probably the one who sabotaged your tire so that you wouldn't show up on time for the meeting."

Emily hadn't told Kevin anything about her relationship with Mark. She said, "You must have discussed this with Mr. Musgrove."

"Yes, Emily. You will remember when I asked you why the FBI was involved in the investigation you said I should ask the FBI. After I left you that day I returned to the crime scene and reviewed the whole thing with Musgrove. The FBI were in charge of the investigation, but they have to have the cooperation of the local police for the basic investigative work. Sergeant Burris left in a huff and I wanted Musgrove to know that regardless of that he had the support of the Los Angeles PD."

Emily was feeling uneasy about this. She thought she was speaking in confidence with Musgrove, but if he needed the support of the local police he would have to cooperate with them. It was a two way street.

"I'll just be a few minutes Kevin, if you'd like some coffee I'll put some on."

"No thanks, I'll just wait."

Emily crammed everything she could into three bags, clothing, shoes, toilet articles, and a couple of books. She would repack everything at Petie's. She wheeled the first bag into the living room; Kevin took the handle and headed for the front door.

"Wait Kevin, I have more."

Emily returned a minute later wheeling one more bag and carrying another.

"You must be intending to stay at Petie's for quite a while."

"Actually," Emily said, "Petie and I are going to take a vacation. I thought I'd take everything over to her place and then sort out what I want to take with me."

"Incidentally Emily, Sergeant Burris told me to tell you that he would like you to stay in town until the investigation is completed."

"And how long will that take, six months, a year? Tell Sergeant Burris that I told you to tell him to go to hell."

Kevin grinned, "In those exact words?"

"In those exact words."

Emily wheeled the largest of the three bags into Petie's apartment building while Kevin carried the other two. When Petie answered the door Emily introduced them.

"I'd like you to meet my friend, Petie Clarkeson," and to Petie she said, "this is Detective Kevin Johnson."

Petie gave Kevin a shy smile and a friendly, "How do you do?"

And in return Kevin gave a slight bow and said, "I'm pleased to meet you."

"Would you like some coffee?" Petie asked.

"I would," Emily replied, "I'm dying; Kevin?"

"Sure, I have a few minutes to spare."

When Kevin asked about their vacation plans Petie gave Emily a sideways look but said nothing. Coffee over Kevin got up to leave.

"I'm pleased to have made your acquaintance Petie, and I hope we meet again some time."

Petie expressed her mutual desire and Emily said, "Kevin, I'll walk you to your car."

"Kevin you've been a good friend. I want to thank you for all you've done." Emily wanted to kiss him on the cheek but she thought she had better keep their relationship on a businesslike basis.

"It's been a pleasure, Emily. And if I can help you with anything else, you still have my phone number." He added, "I'd drive you to the airport but I don't want to be accused of aiding and abetting your escape."

"I hope this won't get you into trouble, Kevin."

"Sergeant Burris will be annoyed, but I'll tell him that, short of arresting you, there was nothing I could do to compel you to stay; and if I arrested you I'd have to charge you with something, and I couldn't think of anything I could charge you with."

Emily extended her hand which he shook warmly and drove away.

Back in the apartment Petie said, "How come you get to meet all the nice looking guys?"

Emily said, "And all the dirty rats."

She went on to explain what she had learned about Mark Sheldon, also known as Michael Shannon.

"I didn't tell you, Petie, because I wasn't sure. When I was interviewed by Agent Musgrove of the FBI, he asked me if I had discussed the meeting with anyone. I told him I had been out with Mark the night before. We were having such a good time Mark didn't want to call it a day. I told him I wanted to get home as I had to attend a meeting at eight a.m. He said that was pretty early for a meeting and I told him that two of the men who were attending the meeting had to catch an early flight. I guess he put two and two together and decided that the meeting was important."

"Do you think he shot all of those people." Petie asked, wide eyed.

"Kevin didn't think so. The theory is that embezzlers and con men usually don't resort to violence. Mark may have passed the information on to the killer, or he may have been working separately on his own. Either way I feel terrible about it. To think that I may have caused the death of all of those innocent people by opening my big mouth."

"I don't think you should speculate that way, Emily. I think the whole thing was just bad luck."

"Thanks, sweetie," Emily replied. "I guess I also feel hurt and let down."

She was thinking of the word 'betrayed' but that might be melodramatic as she had only met him three weeks ago.

"I really liked him. He was handsome and charming and he had a subtle way of giving me little flattering compliments. In the back of my skull somewhere I think there was a little voice saying, 'this may be *the* man.' But there was something about him that made me feel uneasy. When I asked him anything about himself he seemed to clam up or change the subject. I guess he might have felt the same about me. When he asked me about my work I was naturally evasive."

IX

The flight from Los Angeles to Puerto Vallarta was not crowded. Emily and Petie were seated away from other passengers, with relative privacy.

"Petie, I think you realize that we are no longer biologists working on research. Mr. Armitage referred to us as agents, and more loosely as 'Spies.' When you and I were working as biologists there were certain matters about which we were not informed. Because I had more responsibility than you I was given more information than you. The logic behind this was that the less you knew the less chance there was that you might inadvertently leak information that that would be of use to anyone opposed to the work we were engaged in. I'm a pretty good example of this; what I blabbed may have brought about the massacre at the office."

Petie interrupted, "That's not true Emily. There could have been many reasons that we don't know about. And no one has been more hard working and loyal than you have."

"Anyway Petie, now you and I are in is together and it's only fair that you should know the whole story. You may have guessed about what was going on, but I'll give you the whole thing, at least I'll give you all of the important stuff."

"We started almost four years ago. All that I was told was that we were going to produce plant pathogens that would adversely affect the coca plant which is the precursor to cocaine. An operation was set up in the mountains northeast of Los Angeles. We called it the 'farm.' It was very secretive. I worked with Mr. Andrews and Candejar. Without being briefed on the operation I came to the conclusion that the pathogen was going to be used to combat the drug dealers in South America. In time we had produced the pathogen and the next step was to create an efficient method of using it to infect the coca fields."

"About this time someone had got wind of our operation and it was rumored that an inquiry was to be conducted by the EPA. Rather than risk disclosure of the operation it was almost immediately closed down. In the meantime Candejar started up the operation in Mexico. That's where were going now. This was a secret operation, for security reasons the Mexican government wasn't informed. The whole thing was hidden in the jungle, somewhere north of Puerto Vallarta."

The airplane banked to the left on its approach to the Puerto Vallarta airport. Below were miles of pristine beaches and the turquoise waters of the Pacific Ocean washing ashore in long, quiet wrinkles.

From the airport they took a taxi to the De Anza Hotel, a three story structure on a quiet street three blocks from the ocean. It occupied an entire city block. The building had a plain white facade, balconies with wrought iron railings being the only ornamentation.

Massive carved wooden doors led to the lobby which was large and spacious. The ceiling, two stories high, was supported by heavy beams. The lower portions of the walls were paneled in mahogany and the floors were of rich-colored hardwood. A mahogany reception desk took up half of the wall on the left side of the lobby with entry to the hotel restaurant at the front. Glass-paneled doors led to the dining room at the rear of the lobby and elevators and stairway took up the remainder of the rear wall. In one corner of the lobby was a writing room with tables and writing materials for the use of guests.

Furnishings consisted mostly of leather upholstered sofas, wooden side tables with lamps, and the occasional accent chair.

Emily and Petie left their baggage in their room and headed for the restaurant. "We can unpack later." Emily said.

In the restaurant a young man approached; medium height, slight build, straight black hair and deep set brown eyes. He had neat youthful features.

“Miss Smith?”

“I’m Emily Smith,” Emily replied.

“My name is Arturo Martinez. I’m sorry to hear your mother is not well.”

“She’s feeling much better, thank you.”

Arturo Martinez looked younger than the twenty-one years Armitage had attributed to him. He continued to look at Emily intently.

“Is something wrong?” she asked him.

"Excuse me, Senorita, I was not expecting to meet someone so young, and so beautiful."

Actually it seemed strange to him that a woman should be in charge of this kind of operation.

Petie giggled, and Emily said, "Thank you, Arturo, and you can call me Emily." With a hand directed at Petie she said, "This is Petie."

Petie said, "How do you do," and extended her hand.

Petie thought it was sophisticated for a woman to shake hands with a man. Arturo took her hand and shook it carefully; he had never shaken hands with a woman before.

"What strange creatures American women are," he thought.

"Would you like some coffee, Arturo?"

"No, thank you. I just had lunch."

"We've just finished our lunch, Arturo and we'd like to get started right away."

Arturo glanced under the table and noting the high heels that Emily and Petie were wearing replied, "I think you should change your shoes, and maybe put on something to protect your arms and legs. Where we're going the ground is very rough and we will have to walk through the underbrush for quite a distance. The way you are now you will get scratched up quite a bit."

"We were intending to change," Emily said, "we'll meet you in he lobby in fifteen minutes."

"There's one thing I want to explain. . . "

"You can explain it later, when we're on our way."

While changing in their room Emily removed a one-hundred dollar bill from her money belt. That should be enough to cover any current expenses. The rest of the money and their credit cards and documents remained in waterproof compartments of the belt.

She had thirty-five dollars in her wallet, a twenty, a ten and a five. She removed the bills and put them in her shirt pocket and put the hundred in her wallet.

She had memorized the combination of Candejar's safe at the jungle outpost but to make sure, she checked Mr. Armitage's memo and jotted it down on a slip of paper. She slipped the paper into her bra. Emily, feeling somewhat cynical, was thinking that there couldn't be a safer place.

Entering the lobby Emily and Petie wore long pants, long-sleeved shirts, light jackets and sturdy walking shoes.

Arturo was waiting by the entry to the hotel. When he saw them he said, "Ah, much better."

Parked outside was a gray-colored SUV with a man leaning on the front fender and facing the hotel. As they approached he stepped forward and smiled.

Arturo said, "This is Carlos Montoya. He's going to drive us to the site."

Emily was incredulous. "What do you mean, 'he's going to drive us to the site,' who is he?"

"I told you in the restaurant that there was something I wanted to explain. My truck was stolen this morning. I have no transportation. When I told Carlos I had to make a journey today, he offered to help."

"Please excuse us Mr. Montoya. Come over here, Arturo," Emily ordered, and walked out of hearing distance of Montoya. Petie followed.

Emily was furious. She demanded of Arturo, "What's this all about?"

"This morning I parked my truck on the parking lot at the bank. When I came out of the bank my truck was gone. Someone had stolen it. Carlos came out of the bank just behind me. When I told him my truck had been stolen he offered to drive me to the police station so I could report the theft."

"When we left the Police Station I told him I had to make a special trip today to a camp in the jungle; I asked him if I could borrow his vehicle but he refused. He said the roads around here were so bad that if you loaned someone your vehicle you might not get it back in one piece. He would be willing to drive me himself but I would have to pay for it."

"I asked him how much he would charge and he asked me how far the trip was. I told him about eighty miles round trip and he said he would do it for eighty dollars. That's a pretty good price."

"How long have you know him?" Emily asked.

"Like I said, I met him at the bank this morning."

Emily groaned.

"Do you know anything about him personally?"

"Just what he told me himself. He works at one of the marinas, fixing boats and doing odd jobs for the boat owners. I've seen him around; he seems like and honest person to me."

"Let me talk this over with Petie, tell Montoya we'll be with him in a minute." She turned to Petie, "What do you think of him?"

"I think he's kind of cute."

"Oh, for God's sake Petie, I don't care if he's cute or not. Does he look honest or reliable or what?"

Petie, somewhat abashed, glanced over at Montoya. He was tall for a Mexican, almost six feet, even taller than Arturo. He had black hair, and creamy, brown complexion. He had rather large teeth. When he smiled, his smile seemed to dominate his whole face. He wore a loose brown jacket over a brown shirt open at the neck, black pants and black shoes; all were neat and clean.

"Well, he's clean shaven, his clothes are neat and clean. His SUV is old but it looks clean inside and out. I don't know what else you can go by."

Emily looked at her watch. "It's too late to phone Mr. Armitage. If we wait until tomorrow to phone we'll have to reschedule our air flights." Emily paused. "If he wants to accompany us for any reason other than making some money he'll drive us for any price. Suppose we offer to pay him less that the eighty dollars he asked for. If he accepts it then he may be up to something. If he turns it down then he probably only wants to make some money. What do you think?"

"That sounds logical to me."

Emily waved to Arturo to come over. "Tell Montoya were only willing to pay sixty dollars."

Arturo looked doubtful but said, "OK."

Emily and Petie watched as Arturo talked to Montoya. Montoya shook his head. Arturo returned. "He won't do it for less than eighty dollars."

Emily and Petie exchanged glances. Emily said, "OK. Tell him we accept."

X

Arturo sat in the front passenger seat and directed Montoya while Emily and Petie sat in the back.

Petie leaned over to Emily and whispered, "I still think he's cute."

Once out of the downtown area they headed north on a paved highway. The vehicle provided a chorus of squeaks, rattles and groans. The highway, for the most part was reasonably level. There were occasional potholes which Montoya dodged adroitly.

But some of them he missed and the impact with the roadbed sent painful vibrations up the spines of the passengers, and the squeaks, rattles and groans of the SUV protested even more clamorously.

Twenty-five miles out and just ahead the highway veered to the right and started to rise. Arturo pointed to the left and said to Montoya, "Turn off here."

Now they were on a dirt road leading west toward the ocean. The road had a few rough spots but, compared to the pot-holed highway was soft and smooth. Tangled shrubbery grew close to the road, and on each side, exotic tropical trees crowded close and leaned over toward the road, as though begrudging the road the small space it occupied.

They rounded a curve in the road and the azure-blue Pacific Ocean came into view. The breaking surf washed lazily ashore. Miles of pristine beach and not a person in sight. There was a heavy bank of clouds offshore to the southwest but in the immediate area, save for some fleecy clouds, the sky was mostly clear.

Montoya changed gears and put his vehicle into four wheel drive. It plowed unevenly through the soft, heavy sand till it reached the packed sand, wetted by the surf. Montoya, following Arturo's direction, turned right and followed the shoreline. It curved gently to the left for two or three miles and then jutted abruptly out to sea. Before the abrupt change of direction in the shoreline they came to a point where small rocks and gravel had been washed out of the jungle by heavy rains. The wash was wider than a city street and led directly into the jungle, flanked on each side by tangled shrubbery and dense growth of trees.

They turned up the wash and began a gentle climb. The SUV began its chorus of squeaks, rattles and groans, but not as lustily as its performance on the highway. As they proceeded the wash narrowed and its surface became bumpy and rutted. The tall trees began to hang over the wash, blocking out most of the sun's light and creating a twilight effect.

Montoya was hunched over the steering wheel and gripped it tightly with both hands. He was obviously tense.

Petie looked up at the canopy of leaves. "This is getting spooky, Emily."

"Don't worry, Petie, I'm sure we'll be out of here soon."

They drove on, always on an upward incline, the twilight darkened even more. Montoya turned on the headlights of the truck to better illuminate the way and make visible the patches of rock which popped up here and there.

There was light ahead. Suddenly they found themselves in a wide, flat, gravel-covered clearing, without overhanging trees. But there was no sunshine; the blue sky was now hidden by brooding clouds. . . It was better than the darkness of the jungle.

"No wonder it was so dark in there," Arturo observed, "the sun is gone."

"Are we there?" Petie asked.

"No," Arturo replied, "we're only about half way."

"This seems like its a lot farther than you gave me to believe," Montoya commented to Arturo.

"That's only because we are driving slowly. It really isn't that far."

Noticing Montoya's tenseness Arturo said, "Would you like me to drive? I've driven up this wash many times. I know where every rock and rut is."

Montoya replied, "No, I'll drive."

They drove on through the clearing and continued on the wash. The overhanging trees again shut out the light and the gentle slope became more inclined and made wide curves to the left and to the right. At some points it flattened and then continued the climb.

At the same time the road gradually changed from a wash into an arroyo, still flat on the bottom, but cut into the roadbed, exposing gravel sides. The road became rougher and the SUV's symphony of squeak, rattle and groan resumed, with ferocity.

As they drove on a small wash entered from the left and in the distance disappeared into the underbrush. Soon after another wash entered from the right, and farther on another from the left.

Montoya said, "I think if there were no trees here we would find ourselves in a valley with mountain slopes on each side of us. That's why small washes have formed on each side."

Now the grade became steeper and the gravel sides of the arroyo became higher. They came to a deeply rutted section and the SUV alternately lurched and dived its way through. Past this area the arroyo narrowed till the top of the vehicle was lower than the rocky sides of the arroyo. It was like a narrow canyon just wide enough for the truck to pass though.

"Why are there such deep ruts in the road?" Petie asked, "until now it hasn't been too bumpy."

Arturo turned to look at Petie and explained, "The arroyo is so narrow here, and so deep. In the rainy season when we have heavy rains, the runoff of surface water is so great that this whole arroyo is filled with water. Right now, if we were in the arroyo during a rainstorm, our heads would be below the surface of the water. The surge of the water is so great that, if we hadn't already downed, we would be swept down the arroyo and smashed against the rocks."

"Ugh," Petie said, "what would happen to us if it started to rain right now?"

"Don't worry," Arturo replied, "it never rains this time of year."

Up ahead the arroyo disappeared into the underbrush. Montoya stopped.

"Keep going," Arturo urged.

The vehicle crept along till its front bumper touched the underbrush. It could go no farther. But there, on the right, hacked out of the jungle by machete, was a small clearing, big enough for a car or truck, and not visible from fifty feet down the arroyo.

Montoya turned in and parked. From below the parking area could not be seen. Anyone coming this far up the arroyo would assume that it had come to an end and would try to proceed no farther.

"I cleared this myself," Arturo said, with a touch of modest pride.

"Very clever, Arturo," Montoya said, "no one would think of going beyond this point."

Arturo turned to Petie, smiled and said, "Petie, we're here."

Ahead, Arturo had hacked open a narrow path. It was narrow so that their arms and their heads scraped against the branches of the undergrowth. In a few minutes they came to a chain link fence with a chain and padlock on the gate. Arturo produced a key and unlocked the padlock.

"Does this fence surround the whole property?" Emily asked.

"No," Arturo answered, "it just runs into the underbrush about six feet, but it gives the impression that it does."

They continued on through a pathway in the underbrush to a clearing in the jungle, without the canopy of trees overhead. The project consisted of two tents, one small used for sleeping quarters, and the other large, used as a laboratory.

"Crude!" Emily thought.

Though rudimentary, the camp was well designed. The main tent contained all of the necessary laboratory equipment; plexiglass windows faced north to provide adequate unglaring light, and propane gas and an electrical generating plant were adjacent to the tent.

They had refrigeration and cooking facilities, all the comforts of home.

Emily wanted privacy. Before entering the main tent she turned to Arturo and said, "Arturo, why don't you and Mr. Montoya stay out here and keep guard. Let us know if you hear anyone approaching?"

Both men sensed that she preferred to have them wait outside and nodded.

Emily checked the refrigerator first. Empty. Then she started on the safe. She turned to Petie and said, "Petie, while I'm doing this check around and see if there are any papers or records of any kind. He might have left something in his desk."

Emily opened the safe. Inside was the cassette of pathogen that they were specifically looking for. There was also a small vial of pathogen, this apparently being the excess produced after the cassette had been filled. There was also Candejar's daily log book. Emily closed the safe and put the vial of pathogen in her bra.

"Find anything Petie?"

"No, Emily, this was a pretty tidy man."

Outside Emily handed the cassette and log book to Arturo. "Put these in your shirt Arturo, and don't lose them."

"I'll try not to," Arturo responded.

Montoya turned the SUV around in the parking space and proceeded back down the arroyo. He drove carefully over the deeply rutted section, but even so the SUV lurched from side to side. They were still in the deepest part of the arroyo. The top of their vehicle was still lower than the arroyo's sides. Soon it widened and they were back on the flatter, wider area.

As they passed over the end of the flat area and started to slope downward and around a curve another vehicle suddenly came into view. It was a Jeep with two men in it. Emily was aghast when in the passenger seat she recognized the man with slouch hat, the man she had seen in the hallway of her office building, just before she came upon the massacre. The killer!

"That's him!" she shrieked, "the man who killed all of the people at the office." Despite the subdued twilight of the arroyo the man with the slouch hat was still wearing dark glasses.

The two vehicles sped by each other and the occupants of the Jeep were obviously taken by surprise.

Petie looked back. "They've stopped and they're turning around."

Seconds later they heard two shots but both missed. "I think they're shooting at us." Petie cried.

They rounded a curve and the Jeep was out of sight. Coming up on the right was one of the washes they had observed on the way up. Montoya skidded almost to a stop, turned up the wash and accelerated. He didn't stop until a curve in the wash hid them from view from the arroyo. They heard the Jeep pass down the arroyo with a roar.

Montoya put the SUV into reverse and backed recklessly out of the wash and onto the arroyo, with the vehicle facing uphill.

"Why didn't you keep going," Arturo demanded, "we could have outrun them."

"These people aren't stupid," he replied, "they'll have people waiting for us at the bottom of the wash."

Emily thought, "What does he mean, 'these people?' Does he know who they are?" She was beginning to have uneasy feelings about Montoya.

Just then Arturo interrupted her thoughts by asking, "What did you mean, Emily, about him being the killer?"

"I'll explain later, Arturo, right now were in a mess and we have to figure how to get out of it."

To Montoya she said, "Do you have some kind of plan?"

"Yes, the camp can't be more than five or six miles from the highway. If we cut through the jungle we should be able to make it there in about an hour and a half."

Arturo said, "That's about the right distance. When we built the camp we carried most of our materials and equipment through the jungle to avoid the beach where people might observe us and wonder what we were up to. We used wheel barrows and made our own trail. We haven't used it for about three months, but I think I can still follow it."

"We won't have a lot of time to spare." Montoya interposed. "When they get to the clearing and don't see us ahead of them, they'll realize that what we did and they'll turn back. When they get to the camp they'll conclude that we are cutting through the jungle. My guess is that they won't try to follow us through the jungle. They'll go back down the wash, drive around to the highway and try to cut us off."

Emily was feeling more uneasy than ever. This was no odd-job man fixing boats at a marina. He was a shrewd thinker and planner. There was nothing she could do about it now, just keep an eye on him.

XI

The SUV slammed up the arroyo. What they experienced before was nothing like their present ride, tossed violently from side to side, thrown violently upward; all of them held their hands above their heads to prevent the impact of head on roof.

Montoya drove deftly into the parking space. They all piled out of the vehicle; Arturo unlocked the padlock on the gate.

"Quickly, quickly," Montoya admonished, "we don't have any time to spare if we are going to survive."

Emily said, "Arturo, lock the chain on the gate. I know they can get through it, but it might hold them up for a minute."

Inside the tent Emily said, "I'm going to lock the safe."

Montoya asked, "What for?"

"You said we don't have time to spare. They might take a minute or two trying to open it."

Montoya picked up a coil of rope that was on Candejar's desk. He placed it over his head and under on arm so that it was supported by one shoulder and did not restrict the use of his arms. Emily asked, "What do you want that for?"

"When you're in the jungle you never know when rope might come in handy." Emily shrugged.

Outside was the garden of coca plants that Arturo had nurtured through many months, and it was now to be abandoned. He took up his machete with which he had, for so many months protected his garden from encroachment by the jungle, and slashed aimlessly and in frustration at some of his botanical wards.

"All this work for nothing," he said.

Emily put her hand on Arturo's shoulder and said, "All right, Arturo, let's go." Emily understood the frustration he was feeling.

Arturo approached the undergrowth at the side of the garden and was about to start hacking a path through the tangled undergrowth.

Montoya said, "Wait!'

"In case they do decide to follow us into the jungle let's not give them any clue as to where we went through." He surveyed the wall of underbrush and pointed and said, "Here. Give me the machete, Arturo."

Montoya didn't use the machete but used his hands and arms to clear a path and push his way into the underbrush. "Follow me," he said. Emily pushed Petie ahead. None of them really wanted to enter this tangled mess of branches. Emily followed and Arturo took up the rear.

Branches of the undergrowth tore at their arms and legs and vines clung to their feet. When he was six feet into the undergrowth Montoya started to slash with the machete; all were soon able to follow the pathway he had cleared. As they moved into the jungle the canopy of the trees shut out more of the sun's light, the underbrush thinned and soon had all but disappeared.

"If they should decide to follow us," Montoya declared, "they'll have a hard time picking up our trail."

Arturo now took the lead. Following the trail he was familiar with he picked a path around the tall jungle trees with their canopy of leaves far above. Except for the chatter of birds in the canopy , there were no sounds. And deepening twilight instilled a feeling of unease in all. A feeling that they were trespassing in the jungle's private world.

Emily looked at her watch. It would be two hours before the end of day. Why was the creeping darkness becoming so profound?

Then they heard it, the rumble of thunder off in the distance. They continued their march, always on a slight incline. Without the sun to guide them they had no sense of direction.

Emily said to Arturo. "How can you avoid getting lost if you can't tell which direction you're going in? "

"I've developed a sense of direction in here. In any event, if you walk uphill you eventually reach the highway. If you walk downhill you eventually get to the ocean.

Another peal of thunder, but much closer. "We're going to have a storm," Emily said. “Listen!"

"I don't hear anything," Petie whispered.

"That's just it. The birds have stopped singing."

They all looked at one another and the silence was ominous; then the silence was broken by the gentle patter of rain on the high canopy. It happened! A flash of light, a rending crash like giant sheets of paper being torn apart by giant hands, followed by an explosive boom of thunder. Lightning had struck close by.

Then came the rain, falling on the canopy so intensely it sounded like the roar of an airline jet. Rain came down, not in drops but in huge splashes as it washed its way through the leaves. The descending rain was so intense, huddled together they felt that they could hardly breathe.

Arturo had removed his light jacket and draped it over his and Petie's heads. It didn't keep them dry but it did beak the fall of the splashing rain. It rained for five minutes and then as quickly as it had begun it ceased. For this they were all thankful.

They were standing in water up to their ankles. Everywhere they looked there was water. Arturo wrung the water from his jacket and put it back on. The others stood there, wet and soggy, and looked on. Emily felt an urge to scratch but restrained herself. It was the money belt! Not even noticeable when it was dry, it now felt like a girdle of sandpaper around her waist.

Arturo with a smile on his face and a chuckle said, "We look like a bunch of wet hens."

"What is a wet hen?" Petie asked.

"A wet hen is a lady chicken that has been caught in the rain. She doesn't know what to do so she just stands there looking and wet and miserable." And he added, “Like us!”

Petie, with arms bent at the elbow, flapped them like a chicken and, cavorting around said, "Puck, puck, puck; I'm a wet hen, I'm a wet hen," and then added, "now that you've insulted all of us Arturo, what do you propose that we do next?"

"My shoes are full of rain water, so what I propose to do next is take off my shoes and spill out the water." He did, and the others, thinking it was a good idea, followed suit.

"Didn’t you say that it never rained this time of year?" Emily inquired.

"What I meant was," Arturo replied rather abashedly, "it hardly ever rains this time of year."

Montoya, wanting to get back to the problem at hand interjected, "I don't think they followed us. If they did this rain has wiped out any trail or footprints we may have made. If they didn't follow us and they were in the arroyo when the rain started, they're in bad trouble."

"They may have abandoned their vehicle and climbed out of the arroyo, but the arroyo will be flooded and it will take at least an hour for the flood water to clear." Montoya paused. " In any event, we had better push on and get out of here as fast as we can."

A mile farther in their trek and they came to a small stream which cut diagonally across their path. It was only ten or twelve feet wide but the water was flowing at a furious rate. To risk crossing might result in injury or even drowning.

"There's a place where we can cross," Arturo explained, "but it will take us about a half mile out of our way. We have to follow this stream." He led the way.

As he predicted they came to a place where the flood water had spread over a smooth area of rock, thirty or forty feet wide. Still the water was six inches deep and flowed so fast as to make footing unsteady. Arturo led the way, holding Petie by the hand. Emily and Montoya followed. They crossed without mishap and then turned leftward to pick up the original trail.

Arturo stopped. His shoes were again filled with water from having crossed the stream. "I have to get this water out of my shoes," he said.

"All right," Montoya said, "but hurry. We don't want to be in the jungle after dark."

"Why not," Petie inquired, "are there wild animals in here?"

"Just pumas, but a puma wouldn't attack four people."

"What's a puma?" Petie asked.

"A puma is a mountain lion," Emily explained. "We have them in California. We call them mountain lions, down here they call them pumas. But Montoya is right. We don't want to be here in the jungle after dark."

As they hiked on they began to see thinning of the leaf canopy and soon, soft blue sky above. Blue sky! The storm had passed and the weather was now clear. Soon they stepped out of the jungle into the open. The highway was just beyond. They were wet and bedraggled but everyone smiled. Though the sky was clear the sun was hidden by the trees; it would soon be dark.

Despite the dousing from the cloudburst they had survived. Everything seemed to be going well.

"All we have to do now is get a ride into . . ." Emily stopped in the middle of her sentence.

Montoya had removed the coil of rope from his shoulder and stood there with a pistol in his right hand.

"I'm afraid I must part company with you." All of them gaped in disbelief.

"Now if you will please throw your wallets and pocketbooks over here." He indicated a spot on the ground and, still open mouthed, they complied.

"And Arturo, the cassette and the log book ." Arturo removed them from his shirt and tossed them over.

"Empty your pockets please." They did so and out came an assortment of peso notes, dollar bills, change and keys.

"Thank you," said Montoya.

"Now if the three of you will stand back to back." Montoya waved his pistol to remind them of his authority. They did as he directed.

"Take this end of the rope in your hand, Arturo." He did.

"And all of you, drop your hands to your sides."

Montoya walked round and round them, coiling the rope around their bodies till they were thoroughly bound and then he tucked in the loose end.

"I told you a rope might come in handy in the jungle, Emily."

"How can you be so despicable?" Emily almost spit out the words.

Montoya smiled and sorted through the booty on the ground, removing cash and discarding everything else. He put the cassette in his jacket pocket.

He looked at the soggy log book. "This is ruined," he said and tossed it aside.

"Your one-hundred-dollar bill, Emily," he said as he removed it from her wallet. "I'll send you twenty dollars change."

"You only brought us halfway, so you should also refund half of the eighty dollars."

"The excursion was truncated by circumstances beyond my control," Montoya laughed, "so you get no refund for that."

He continued to sort through the booty.

"Funny," he said, "no credit cards, no passports, and only one hundred dollars in Emily's wallet. Maybe you left something behind somewhere?"

No doubt he was thinking of their hotel room. They would probably find it ransacked when they got back. Despite the itching Emily was now thankful for the money belt around her waist.

"How do you expect to get back to town?" Emily asked.

"As you say in the United States, I will thumb a ride. And as an incentive to any motorist who comes by I will place this fifty peso note that I took from Arturo's wallet between my thumb and my forefinger." He held it up for them to see.

"And now, I think you'll be more comfortable sitting down."

With this he gave Arturo a hearty shove. The bundled three lurched and staggered and finally fell to the ground in an undignified manner. Now they sat among the small bushes that dotted the highway clearing.

Montoya roared with laughter. “If only you could see how funny you looked, staggering around like a group of drunks. That has been the highlight of the afternoon for me. A scene that I will cherish forever.”

Montoya strode off towards the highway, and then he stopped and turned.

“Incidentally Arturo, you'll find your Toyota truck parked on the street behind the Catholic Church. When you went into the bank I parked it on the next street. When you came out I pretended that I had left the bank just behind you and I told you I had seen someone drive away in it. I drove you to the police station and after you had made your report I dropped you off at your hotel.

Then I returned and picked up the Toyota and parked it behind the church. The police never go there."

As Montoya departed Arturo said "Very clever, Montoya." And the way he said it left no doubt as to his negative feelings toward Montoya.

Montoya was soon out of sight, screened by the small bushes around them.

"Damn it," Emily said, "I've done it again. First I get everyone in the office massacred, and now I let myself be duped by another crook."

"Tell me what this is all about," Arturo demanded, "you mentioned that the man we saw in the Jeep was a killer, and now you're talking about a massacre. What does it all mean?"

Petie turned her head and spoke quietly into his ear, "Not now, Arturo."

Arturo didn't pursue his question but continued.

"It wasn't your fault, Emily. I was the one who was duped by Montoya. If it wasn't for my stupidity you never would have met him."

"Thank you Arturo, but I'm in charge of this secret, clandestine operation. Some secret! The man with the slouch hat knew about it; Michael Shannon, alias Mark Sheldon new about it; and now this Carlos Montoya pops up out of nowhere, and he knows about it.

Whoever is in charge of keeping secrets has sure screwed up."

Arturo started to ask, "Who is . . . " But Petie again turned her head and whispered in his ear, "Quiet."

In the distance they heard an approaching truck, then a squeal of brakes as it stopped; and then it started up.

"There goes Mr. Montoya," Emily stated.

"Thanks to my fifty-peso note," Arturo added.

"All right," Emily said, "enough of my whimpering. We have to figure out how to get out of here."

She continued. "We can't do anything sitting here on our butts, so let's get upright. Pull your knees up to as close as you can to your chests." They did.

"Now, push on your feet as hard as you can." The three of them did and with gasps and grunts acquired an upright stance. They were still bound tightly by the rope coiled around them.

"Petie, you're elected to get us loose."

"How?" Petie inquired.

"Arturo, you're going to twist your body away from Petie and I'll twist my body away from Petie. That will give her a little breathing space. And Petie, when you feel you have some space start twisting your torso from side to side and let your body drop at the same time. Ready?"

"Yes."

"All right Arturo, twist as hard as you can."

The two pulled away from Petie who started to twist from left to right and right to left, and let her body slip downward. As she did so she let out little noises, halfway between a murmur and a grunt. Down she went, half an inch at a time.

"You're doing great, Petie!" Emily exclaimed.

Petie, with knees now bent, had to grasp the legs of Emily and Arturo for leverage, finally she dropped to the ground on her knees and the coils of rope that held the three fell with her.

Arturo helped her up and Emily gave her a hug. "What would we ever do without you, Petie?" she said.

"We'll have to flag down a ride," Emily said as they reached the highway.

"It would help if we had my fifty peso note," Arturo complained.

Emily triumphantly produced the money from her shirt pocket. "Do you think this will do?" she asked as she peeled off a five dollar bill.

"You're a clever lady, Emily." Arturo said.

"I tell her that all of the time," Petie added, "but she's so modest I don't think she believes me."

"There's a truck coming," Petie said, "but it's coming from town."

"Montoya said the people who were after us might come back around to the highway and try to cut us off. We had better hide."

They hurried back to the safety of the jungle. The truck drove by without slowing down.

A few minutes later a truck came from the north, heading for Puerto Vallarta. Emily waved her five dollar bill and the driver of the truck, seeing it, came to a stop.

Petie and Arturo jumped into the back of the truck and Emily climbed up beside the driver, she handed him the five dollar bill.

"Gracias Senorita." He asked her a question in Spanish to which Emily shrugged and said, "No comprendo Espanol, Senor." At least she wouldn't have to try to explain what the three of them were doing stranded on the highway, miles from Puerto Vallarta.

He dropped them off at their hotel. Arturo said, "I'm going to get my truck."

"Why didn't you ask him to drive you over there?" Emily inquired.

"It's only about six blocks. I should be back in about ten minutes."

"Meet us in the lobby in about forty-five minutes."

XII

As Emily and Petie walked through the hotel lobby to the elevator, wet and bedraggled, guests in the hotel stared.

"We were caught in the rain," Petie tried to explain to one of the guests, but Emily grasped her by the elbow and propelled her on toward the elevator.

When they entered their room they found it in disarray. The beds had been taken apart, all of their clothing had been scattered onto the floor. Emily's computer case lay open on its side on the desk.

Emily checked the computer case first. "He took my notes," she said resignedly." But they're in my computer so I can reproduce them when we need them."

"I wonder why he didn't take your computer?" Petie asked.

"He probably figured that if he were stopped he would have a hard time explaining where he got the computer. It won't compute without the password and he'd wouldn't be able to explain why he couldn't get it to run."

“Do you think it was Montoya, for sure?” Petie asked. “Maybe it was one of the men in the Jeep. We really don’t know what happened to them.”

They straightened out the beds and sorted through the mess of clothing, arranging it neatly on the beds as they went along.

Petie pointed to the mirrror on the wall and said, “Look, Emily!” Taped to the mirror was a twenty-dollar bill.

“Now we know for sure who was in here. And Montoya can’t be all bad, just ninety-nine point nine per cent.”

“Have you noticed anything else missing?”

“No,” Petie giggled, “I guess I don’t have anything worth stealing.”

“All he was looking for was my notes and money. He got my notes but they can be replaced. And thank God for the money belt.”

Her statement reminded her how irritating the money belt had become. Off came her shoes, shirt and pants, and with a smile and a flourish she ripped off the Velcro- fastened belt. Now she was able to check it. Passports, credit cards and money, all were safe and dry.

“You know, Petie, I thought the money belt thing was being a little melodramatic, but now I realize how important it was. If we had lost all of our money and credit cards and documents, think what a mess we’d be in.”

Petie nodded her approval and said, “Emily, someday you’ll turn out to be a good spy!”

Emily put a gentle fist to Petie’s chin and said, "You brat! Show a little respect for your elders!"

After being soaked in the rain a hot shower was a resuscitation of the spirit. It wasn't just being soaked to the skin and terrified by lightning and thunder, it was the cavalier treatment by Montoya that was so demeaning.

Petie flopped out on her bed. "If I wasn't so hungry I'd just lie here for two days. After that soaking I don't even feel like going outside again."

"Let's go Petie, Arturo will be waiting.

“It’s all so unfair,” Petie complained, “ women always have to look their best and men just put on their clothes and brush their hair and they’re done.”

“So, would you like to go casual or dress up?” Emily asked.

“Let’s wear the dresses we bought for our debut at the Embassy. After what we’ve been through today we owe it to ourselves to put on a little class.”

Fifteen minutes later the elevator opened and two classy ladies in elegant dresses and high heels made their entrance into the hotel lobby. No one recognized them as the bedraggled wrecks that had passed through the lobby forty-five minutes earlier.

Emily was right. Arturo was waiting. He rose as they approached.
“You look beautiful!” he was looking at Petie, but he glanced at Emily and quickly added, “Both of you.”

Arturo was wearing a sports coat and shirt and tie. With his youthful appearance he looked quite handsome. Petie's eyes gave her unspoken approval.

"Thank you from both of us," Emily grinned and asked, "was your room searched?"

"No, it was just as I had left it. I guess he probably figured I didn't have anything worth stealing."

"They went through our room and made a mess," Petie said.

"There wasn't any damage, just clothes strewn about and the beds turned inside out, but after the miserable afternoon it was a heavy burden on our already tired shoulders." Petie liked to dramatize a bit.

"They took my notes, but I can reproduce them so it isn't a great loss." Emily paused and then added, "I don't know why we're saying 'they.' We all know it was Montoya who did it. The only bad part of it is that he might be able to use the notes in some way that would work against what we're trying to do."

Unlike the slightly glitzy restaurant the dining room was quiet and reserved. The walls were paneled with mahogany, floors were carpeted and the ceiling was artistically beamed. There was a massive crystal chandelier in the center of the room. Traditional gilt-framed paintings adorned the walls.

Larger linen-covered tables filled the center of the dining room and smaller tables took up the perimeter next to the walls. Each side table was lighted by a separate table lamp.

The dining room was not crowded. Only half a dozen tables were occupied. The maitre d' clicked and a waiter hurried over and showed them to a table in the center of the dining room.

"We would prefer a table by the wall," Emily instructed the waiter. It was essential that they have a quiet place where they could talk over the day's events.

Menus were provided and the waiter inquired as to whether they would like wine.

"Why not?" Emily said and ordered the wine suggested.

Looking at the menu Arturo said, "This place is very expensive."

"Dinner is on us," Emily said, "or should I say, on Mr. Armitage. But don't get used to it. We're only doing this to make up for the nasty time we had this afternoon. Tomorrow it's tortillas and beans."

Emily felt a little celebration was in order. They were all feeling a little dejected after their episode with Montoya. And besides, Mr. Armitage hadn't given any instructions about expenses. She felt a little uneasy when she thought about him. What would he say when he found out how she had been duped? Again?

They began to recount the events, the scary ones came first; the chase on the arroyo, the spookiness of the jungle, the thunderstorm with its buckets of rain, and Montoya with his pistol pointed at them.

"Do you think he would have shot us?" Petie asked.

"If we had tried to overpower him, he would have," Arturo stated, "but I don't think he would have wanted to." He added, "I'm sorry about that, Emily. I should have realized he was a phony."

"*I* should have realized he was a phony, Arturo. My biggest problem on my mind right now is having to explain it to Mr. Armitage tomorrow. I don't know what he'll say. But I'll deal with that tomorrow. Let's enjoy our dinner."

"Something you should know about Petie, Arturo. She's a dedicated optimist; and if she can find anything positive or funny in a situation, she'll find it. Remember after the storm we were all standing there soaked to the skin and feeling miserable, Petie went into her chicken act. Even Montoya was laughing."

"And when we were all bundled up by Montoya, and he gave us a shove, and we staggered around like a bunch of drunks! No wonder he was amused," Arturo added.

Petie piped up, "I think the funniest part of the whole day was when we of us walked through the lobby, all bedraggled and soaking wet. And everyone in the lobby turned and stared. And I could see those blank expressions on their faces, as though they didn't believe what they were seeing."

“Well,” Emily added, “as a compliment to ourselves, I don’t think anyone recognized us when we walked into the lobby tonight.”

“Arturo,” Emily asked, “what about your truck?”

"It was there, just as Montoya said. I drove it back over here. I guess I'll have to tell the police tomorrow that I found it."

Addressing Arturo, Emily said, "You speak very good English, Arturo. How did you learn?"

"In high school I was doing very poorly in English. My English teacher stopped me one day after class. He told me that proficiency in English would open doors for me. He said, 'Look around you, the men who have nice cars, and nice clothes, and nice girls, all of them speak good English.' It didn't take long for this to seep through my thick skull. I knew he was right. The greatest motivation was the reference to 'nice girls.' Nice girls come first, then cars and clothes."

"From then on I studied English with a passion. I continued with English in college, I have two years of college. And that's how I was chosen for the work with Mr. Candejar. They were looking for a Mexican national with a knowledge of English. It was only a six month contract, but it was an opportunity for me."

"It was exciting, being part of a clandestine operation. I wasn't given all of the details, just that it would thwart the drug trade."

"We couldn't use the arroyo for fear of being observed so we had to carry everything in by hand. Candejar and I would take a truckload of materials and supplies to a point we had selected on the highway. If there was no traffic, or anyone in sight we would pull off the highway and hide the truck in the undergrowth. We had two wheelbarrows, and we hand-carried everything in. We figured it was about five and a half miles."

"That was the interesting part. But after we had set up and got into the routine work it was deadly dull. If we needed anything we didn't have one of us, we took turns, would leave at the crack of dawn and drive down the arroyo before anyone was awake. That way we wouldn't be observed. We would stay in Puerto Vallarta overnight and leave before dawn in the morning. I hated the routine, but I was earning about five times as much as I could have anywhere else."

The same thing that she had been hooked by, Emily mused, *money!*

Dinner over Emily said, "We have to get an early start tomorrow. I'll phone Mr. Armitage at seven, that'll be nine o'clock their time. Our flight leaves at ten so we'll have to be at the airport by nine."

XIII

There was a knock on the door. It was Arturo. "You said you wanted to get started early."

"Come in, Arturo. I have to phone Mr. Armitage and then we can go to breakfast."

Emily dialed and was soon connected with Armitage. She related the happenings of the previous afternoon.

"All of you are all right?" he asked.

"Yes, we were just a bit demoralized."

"And you still have a small amount of pathogen?"

"Yes, it was in a vial in Candejar's safe. I emptied my bottle of vitamin pills and put the contents of the vial it in the bottom. Then I covered the pathogen with pills."

"That should work. The Colombians are more intent on what's going out of their country than on what's coming in." He added, "Make sure you throw the pills away after you get to Bogota."

"Yes Sir."

"How much of a setback will the loss of the cassette be?"

"I think four or five weeks, depending on whether a supply of coca leaves is available."

"All right, then carry on as originally planned."

"I didn't report the robbery to the police. I thought they would ask more questions than we would want to answer."

"You did right, Emily. We'll check out this Montoya and see if we can catch up with him later."

"There's one thing that's been bothering me, Mr. Armitage. This is a clandestine operation, yet so many people seem to know about it, the latest being Montoya."

"Yes, I apologize for that Emily. There's a leak somewhere in our organization. We're starting a new security policy and we hope that will plug up the leaks. I'm pushing very hard on this and I think it is now beginning to sink in, that this operation could be totally devastating to the illegal drug trade. Is there anything else?"

"No Sir."

"I'll leave further instructions for you at the Embassy. I've arranged that you will deal directly with the Ambassador. He will give you his full cooperation." He hung up.

Emily turned to Petie and Arturo. "He apologized! I was expecting him to chew me out for losing the pathogen and he apologized for the breakdown in security."

Emily was pleased. Recalling Agent Musgrove's comment that this was treated as a Mickey Mouse operation, she was now more content in thinking that someone in Washington gave a damn.

They checked out after breakfast and were heading for the doorway when Arturo said, “Stop!”

An SUV had pulled up outside and four men piled out. One of them was the man with the slouch hat.

“Quick,” Emily said, “we’ll hide out in the writing room.” They hurried over to the writing room in the corner of the lobby where they could not be seen.

The man with the slouch hat and one of his three accomplices stopped at the reception desk. They spoke to the desk clerk for a moment and then turned and left the hotel.

“We should have known they’d be looking for us,” Emily said. “While they’re checking out hotels we’ll get to the airport and board our plane.”

They clambered into a taxi and in a few minutes were approaching the airport terminal.

Arturo again said, “Stop!” and ordered the driver to pull over.

“Get down,” he said to Emily and Petie. “The four of them are standing guard in front of the terminal.”

"Do you think they'd bother us with all of these people around?" Petie asked.

"They've already killed five, and maybe six," Emily said. "And when they were shooting at us in the arroyo, just because they missed doesn't mean they weren't trying to kill us. We can't take a chance. Let's get out of here and we'll try to figure out what we should do."

Following instructions the driver pulled back into the traffic flow and they left the airport.

"Where is your truck, Arturo? And how far to the next airport that can connect us with Mexico City?"

"My truck is on the parking lot at the marina and I think Guadalajara would be our best bet. It's about two hundred miles from here."

Emily groaned. "I guess we'll be heading for Guadalajara. I'll phone Armitage and tell him of our change in plans. There are two flights to Bogota from Mexico City. One in the morning and one in the afternoon. If all goes well we should be able to catch the early flight tomorrow."

XIV

As their airplane approached the Bogota airport below, they saw wide streets lined with lush green trees, many parks with open spaces.

In the airport waiting room they were approached by a well dressed man in a business suit.

"Miss Smith?" he inquired.

"Yes, I'm Emily Smith."

"How do you do? I'm Peter Quinn from the Embassy."

"Do you have identification?" Emily was being cautious.

"Of course." Quinn replied and produced his ID for examination.

"I'd like you to meet Petula Clarkeson and Arturo Martinez."

All shook hands and Quinn stated, "I have a limousine waiting. The Ambassador is in Washington. He sends his greetings."

Emily was puzzled. Armitage said they would be dealing directly with the Ambassador. Now Quinn said the Ambassador is in Washington

He continued. "It was suggested that we go first to the Embassy so that we could determine your needs and start setting up a workplace for you. If you prefer, of course, I can take you to your hotel and pick you up later."

"We're anxious to get started. We had better go to the Embassy first." Emily informed him.

While their baggage was being loaded into the trunk of the limo Emily, still gun shy, took the opportunity to check the vehicle license plate and noted the it had a diplomat designation.

Underway, Petie whispered to Emily, "This is fun. I've never ridden in a limousine before."

Emily gave her a little hug. "Petie, you're priceless."

From the airport they passed through a business district and then onto a wide boulevarded street. The limousine stopped for a signal light. A main thoroughfare entered from the left, forming a 'T' intersection.

Quinn informed them, "The street you see to your left leads directly to the Simon Bolivar Hotel where, I understand, you will be staying."

"This is a lovely city," Petie stated.

"Yes," Quinn agreed, "it is. And I hope you will find some leisure to time to explore it. I know you have come here to work, but let's hope that they don't keep you working seven days a week."

The signal light changed and the limousine drove quietly on. There was a large open park to the right. An iron railing separated the park from the street. Children were playing while their parents looked on. Vagrants slept, bundled in blankets on the ground, oblivious to the world around them.

"Just like the USA," Emily thought.

Emily wondered whether she should bring it up or wait until she was alone with Quinn. She decided that, although she was in charge, the three of them were in this together. There was no reason why they shouldn't know what was going on. So Emily continued.

"Mr. Quinn, we were told that we would be dealing directly with the Ambassador, now we find he isn't here. I'm sure there's a credible explanation, if not we'll have to contact our director in Washington for clarification."

"I can understand your concern, Miss Smith. My understanding is that the Ambassador was called to Washington because of the tragedy that occurred in Los Angeles involving your business associates and the two Colombian visitors. This has caused great concern."

"But I'm wondering if this is the best place to discuss this?" he added.

He was referring, of course, to the presence of Petie and Arturo.

Emily replied, "The three of us here in this limousine, Mr. Quinn, have been through a hell of a time together. And now we're a team . . . if there ever was a team, we're it."

And Emily's statement made them a team. Until now they were just three persons, each working toward a common end. But in her brief statement Emily had established a camaraderie that bound them together with a purpose. “All for one and one for all.”

"Well," Quinn said, taken a little aback by the passion in Emily's declamation, "I meant no offense to you, Miss Clarkeson or to you, Mr. Martinez, but we, in the diplomatic service, are required to follow protocol. Protocol, in the present circumstance suggests that I should discuss this with you in private, Miss Smith, and not in the presence of your subordinates."

He continued, "If you hold yourselves out as a team, then I'm quite content to discuss this with you as a team."

"Thank you, Mr. Quinn," Emily replied, "we appreciate your frankness."

Quinn continued, "The massacre in Los Angeles created an uproar. We were aware, of course, that there was a program designed to wage biological warfare against the drug dealers. But none of us paid much attention, chiefly because we had not received any definitive information. It was just a hazy, nebulous idea without anything in fact to back it up. But now, considering the brutality of the occurrence it was concluded that the drug people must be greatly concerned. And if they were greatly concerned then we obviously should be giving it more attention."

He continued. "The Ambassador will likely be in Washington for three or four days. Of course his time will not be devoted entirely to this matter. He hasn't been to Washington for several months and there are undoubtedly other matters that will need his attention. In the meantime, our instructions are to cooperate with you and help you in any way we can. Edward Gorman is second in command here, and you will be dealing directly with him until the Ambassador returns."

The limousine came to a stop at a stop sign and waited until pedestrians passed over into the park. To the right was the main entry to the park, with masonry columns flanking the entry. A wide, tiled walk led to a high fountain with water cascading down to a pool. The sound of the tumbling water couldn't be heard within the limo, but the aesthetic value of the scene was not lost.

The Embassy compound was surrounded by a six foot masonry wall with additional metal grillwork on top providing an effective barrier to anyone who would want to enter without permission. A military guard was stationed the gate and saluted as it swung open. A circular driveway led to the front of the Embassy building and then back to the gate. In the center of the circle was a white flagpole with the American flag snapping smartly in the crisp breeze.

The embassy building was elegant yet functional. A wide stone stairway led to double doors inlaid with sections of leaded glass. There were leaded glass panels flanking each of the doorways. The entry opened into the main hallway with its marble floors and richly paneled walls. A high vaulted ceiling accommodated a wide marble stairway leading to second floor rooms. The Ambassador's office was off the left side of the hallway and on the right, a doorway led to a large conference room.

Quinn led them into the conference room and asked them to be seated. "I'll tell Mr. Gorman you're here."

As he was leaving Emily said, "Mr. Quinn!" He stopped. "You've been very considerate, we appreciate that."

Quinn smiled, "It's been a pleasure Miss Smith."

XV

A few minutes later a classy, well-dressed lady entered carrying a tray with mugs of hot coffee and slices of fine-grained cake. She placed it on the glass coffee table in front of the guests.

"I'm Mr. Gorman's secretary," she said, as she poured coffee into cups. She had perfect makeup and curly dark-brown hair.

“You weren't asked but I knew you would appreciate a cup of coffee and a snack after your long trip. Mr. Gorman will be here in a few minutes."

Petie said, “My, you have beautiful hair.”

The secretary smiled, said, “Thank you,” and left.

Emily said, “She’s wearing a wig.”

"I'm beginning to like this place already," Arturo said and took a bite of cake and a sip of coffee. "Mmm, good."

"That's called pound cake," Petie volunteered.

Gorman's secretary returned and, addressing Emily said, “This just came for you." It was a package from Armitage.

When she had left Petie said. “You’re right, Emily, she is wearing a wig.”

Petie, always helpful as well as curious helped Emily tear open the package. Emily dumped the contents onto the coffee table. Six floppy disks fell out. Emily looked inside he package and removed a letter. She scanned the letter briefly and said to Petie and Arturo. "We'll review this later, *together*."

Emily emphasized the *together*.

Quinn, although courteous and polite, was a bit stiff and formal. They were not expecting a change from formal to friendly. And then Edward Gorman entered the conference room.

"Well, well, well, what have we here?" An enormous smile dominated his countenance and his blue eyes sparkled. "I was expecting to see three old, timeworn spies, and now I see a handsome young man and two charming young ladies. All of you look like you're just out of college."

He shook hands with each of them in turn, "Miss Smith, Miss Clarkeson, Mr. Martinez." Arturo rose to shake hands and Petie giggled.

Emily said, "All of us would feel more comfortable if you called us by our first names, Mr. Gorman; I'm Emily, this is Petie, and this is Arturo."

"First names are my first choice, but the Ambassador is a stickler for protocol as you may have learned from Mr. Quinn, who is, by the way, also a protocol advocate. So what we'll do is this, if no one is in earshot we'll use first names, otherwise it will be Miss and Mister. By the way, my name is Edward, but you can call me Eddie."

That certainly broke the ice. There were smiles all round.

Gorman was about fifty, medium height and broad shouldered. He had a shock of sandy brown hair, parted at the left and slightly untidy. Except for an abundance of freckles his facial skin was clear and well tanned. His posture was erect and he moved with athletic ease.

He didn't immediately get to the business at hand but reviewed with them their experiences of the last few days. Arturo was wide-eyed when he learned of the massacre at Los Angeles. It had been alluded to in conversations with Emily and Petie, but it was only now that the horror of the incident was openly discussed.

"It was no wonder Emily hadn't wanted to talk about it," Arturo thought.

"I hate to interrupt," Arturo said, "I can understand what happened at Emily's office, but the man named Sheldon, who died in Emily's apartment, how did he fit into all of this? And if he mentioned someone named WANDA, who was Wanda, and how did she fit in?"

Emily answered, "They're still looking into it, Arturo. Sheldon may have been an accomplice of the man with the slouch hat who chased us in the arroyo."

Petie said, "He was a dirty rat."

Gorman cleared his voice and continued with his friendly inquiry. "Emily," he asked, "how did you become involved in this operation?"

"I was just out of college, I majored in biology. The Department of Agriculture was advertising for a biologist and I applied. When I was interviewed I learned that, if hired, I would actually be working for the

Drug Enforcement Administration and work would be carried out clandestinely in a remote location. It all sounded exciting and the salary was much greater than I could earn elsewhere, so I took the job. I worked there for three years, then the operation was shut down and we moved to an office in Los Angeles. We had been there for six months."

"The work was interesting, but I have to admit that if it weren't for the high salary I probably wouldn't have stuck with it. I think Arturo had a similar experience."

Arturo nodded, "I was also attracted by the salary. I would be making five times as much as I could make anywhere else in Puerto Vallarta. It was exciting at first, working on a secret project. After a month the isolation got to me. It became deadly dull and I hated it. But I had only a six month contract so there was light at the end of the tunnel. From what I know now I believe that it was only a stopgap operation, until they could set up in Colombia."

"What about you, Petie?"

"I just started working with Emily about six months ago when the Los Angeles office was opened. I didn't know anything about the clandestine stuff. No one told me officially but from the chit-chat in the office I knew that we were working on something important, something to do with the illegal drug trade. Emily was great to work for and she taught me so much. I was more that satisfied with everything until . . . until all of those terrible shootings."

Gorman looked at his watch. More than an hour had gone by and there had been no mention of the business at hand.

"It's time for lunch. I usually eat in the kitchen when the Ambassador is not here. If that's all right with you," he added.

No one objected and they all rose and headed for the kitchen. The entry to the kitchen was under the stairs but Gorman stopped them and said, "Let me show you to the dining room first."

The dining room was at the back of the hallway. The entry was next to the stairs. The main feature of the dining room was, of course, the dining table, a long and flawless mahogany surface surrounded by twenty or more chairs. Carpeted floors, paneled walls and a beamed ceiling provided an elegant but not uncommon look.

They walked through the dining room. At the far end and to the right, a doorway led to the kitchen.

The kitchen was spacious with an abundance of cupboards, counters and cooking equipment.

Petie whispered to Emily, "This kitchen is bigger than my whole apartment."

Gorman introduced them to the cook. "Greta," he said, "these are our guests from the United States and from Mexico. I invited them to have lunch in your kitchen."

Greta was middle aged, slightly plump and had a round, rosy face. She was obviously pleased to have guests in her kitchen. If they ate in the dining room all she was required to do was to cook while a maid served *her* food to guests. In the kitchen she served the food herself and listened to the appreciative 'oo's' and 'aah's.'

Lunch over, the guests thanked Greta for a delicious meal and left the building by a doorway off the kitchen.

This part of the compound was spacious, bigger than a football field. It was enclosed by the same six foot masonry wall and metal grillwork as at the front area. There was a solid steel door in the far corner and this was wide enough to permit passage of a motor vehicle. Most of the area was planted in lawn surrounded by flower beds and decorative shrubbery. Gorman led them to the far right.

"We're going to remove the lawn and shrubbery in this area. You can set up your coca garden here. We need to know how much space you will need before we start ripping out."

"Arturo can advise you on that, Eddie." Emily said. "He has been appointed gardener for the operation."

Arturo said, "I have?"

"Yes Arturo, you were appointed by me." Emily explained.

Back in the conference room, Gorman informed them, "The Ambassador has received instructions, I assume from your principals Emily, that we are to conduct a raid on one of the coca fields in order to obtain plants for transplanting, and for foliage for you to commence your pathogenic extraction process."

He addressed Emily. "I understand, Emily, that you have received a directive in this regard?"

"Yes Eddie, a letter came just after we arrived here. I was only able to glance through it. But it seemed to correspond to the action you describe. Part of the operation will be to remove coca plants for transplanting. That will be the start of our growing operation here at the Embassy. We'll need about one hundred containers, plant pots, to put the plants in after they have been dug up. The second part will be to cut off the whole plants above ground and remove the cuttings so that we'll have something to start to work with."

"But it would take the three of us, Petie and Arturo and I, a week or more to do this by ourselves."

"Don't worry about that, Emily, The soldiers who take part in the raid will supply all of the help you need."

"The soldiers will need machetes to cut with and twine to bundle the cuttings with. And, of course, they'll need shovels."

"I'll have a list prepared," Gorman said.

"Just one more thing, Eddie, we'll need a freezer chest to store coca leaves in, and a supply of plastic bags, about one gallon size. And we'll need some kind of work table, like a picnic table and some chairs,"

"You want a freezer chest big enough to hold all of the cuttings?"

"No, Eddie, just the leaves. That's the tedious part. Once we get the cuttings back here we'll have to remove leaf after leaf until all of the cuttings have been stripped. As we strip the leaves we'll bag them and freeze them, and they'll be available when we're ready to use them."

Gorman was thinking that this young lady was pretty good at giving orders. He was more accustomed to giving orders rather than receiving them. To make this clear he said, "Emily, although you are in charge of the establishment of your biologic operation, you understand that I will be in charge of the raid on the coca field?"

"Of course, " Emily replied, "My troops and I are completely under your command."

Gorman, feeling that his authority was not being usurped, let out a hearty laugh. "All right, youngsters, permission to leave is granted. The limo will take you to your hotel and I'll see you in the morning. Be here at eight o'clock sharp." He added, "The Ambassador will be back the day after tomorrow and I understand you will be the guests of honor at dinner."

XVI

The Simon Bolivar Hotel was similar in structure to the De Anza in Puerto Vallarta, but much larger. It was a six story building with plain white facade, adorned by balconies with iron railings overhanging the street. The lobby was spacious but had tile instead of hardwood floors and had less elaborate paneling on the walls.

The rooms were comfortable and nicely furnished. Emily and Petie shared a room and Arturo had a room down the hall. They arranged to meet in the lobby in one hour. That would give them time to shower and dress.

Arturo was waiting in the lobby and he rose as the two classy young ladies approached him. They were wearing the same dresses as they wore at the De Anza, and Arturo thought they looked just as stunning. Emily and Petie had agreed, in the interest of practicality, to limit themselves to one dress-up dress. The thought was that since they would not likely be spending more than one night in any one place that no one, other than themselves, would be aware that this was their only dress-up wardrobe.

The dining room, although not as elegant as the De Anza, was more than adequate.

When the waiter came with menus and asked if they wished to order wine, Emily declined.

Arturo asked, "Is it tortillas and beans tonight, Emily?"

Emily answered, "Oh, what the hell, why should we treat ourselves like second class citizens? The taxpayers eventually foot the bill, and we're taxpayers."

"Emily, I've never heard such perfect rationalization," Petie observed.

Emily signaled to the waiter. When he arrived she inquired, "Which wine do you recommend?"

* * *

They were up early the next morning, and they wore the same work clothes they had worn on their fateful day in the jungle. The sopping wet clothes had been hung to dry overnight, but their itinerary didn't permit time for laundering.

"Maybe this wasn't so bad," Emily thought. "At least we won't look as though we've never been out of downtown Los Angeles before."

They climbed into the first taxi that waited in front of the hotel. "American Embassy," Emily instructed. The driver turned and gave her a blank look. Obviously he didn't understand English.

"OK Arturo," Emily said, "give it to him in Spanish,"

Arturo repeated the instructions to the driver in Spanish, but without result. He gave Arturo the same blank look.

Getting down to the one-word strategy of communication, Arturo repeated, "Embajada, Embajada!"

A light turned on in the driver's eyes. "Oh! Si, si," he said, "Embajada, Embajda!"

The taxi took off in a roar. They drove down streets they had not seen before. It soon became apparent that they were not heading for their hoped for destination. They were becoming apprehensive. Were they being kidnapped? It didn't seem likely that this confused driver was a kidnapper. But maybe that was just an act.

Emily was considering what action they should take when the driver brought the taxi to a screeching stop before a gate of iron railings, flanked by masonry columns. A uniformed guard barred their further progress. The sign above the gate indicated that this was the Libyan Embassy.

The smiling taxi driver proudly repeated, "Embajada, Embajada."

Arturo spoke to the guard who was able to converse in Spanish. The taxi driver was Middle Eastern and spoke no Spanish. This was his first day as a taxi driver. He had been to the Libyan Embassy before. He didn't know that there were other embassies so, naturally he took them to the Libyan Embassy. The guard gave the driver detailed instructions on how to get to the American Embassy and they were again on their way.

When they arrived at the gate of the American Embassy, Gorman was waiting for them with a Jeep. He was obviously agitated.

"Emily," he said, "You're twenty minutes late. Timing is crucial in this kind of operation."

Emily explained what had happened and Gorman calmed down. "I should have sent the limo for you," he concluded.

They clambered into the Jeep and sped around the side of the embassy building. In the open area at the rear a helicopter was parked, with the pilot ready to take off. They were quickly seated and, with safety belts fastened, were airborne with a roar of the engine and the beat-beat-beat of the propellers.

XVII

Once airborne and headed for their destination Gorman explained his concern and apologized for his agitation.

"I was upset when you didn't arrive on time. I realize that the delay was not your fault and I apologize for my brusqueness. It is vitally important that we arrive at the coca field at the same time as the soldiers do. The group that is supporting this operation today are highly trained in hit and run operations. They are Commandos, the Colombian equivalent of our Navy Seals or Rangers."

"We are foraging into territory in which rebel insurgents are a potent force. We will have one platoon of thirty men to provide protection and help with the foraging of the coca field. The rebels are no match for these troops. They won't attack unless they have superiority in numbers of three or four to one."

"When soldiers arrive the farmer who owns the field will flee. He will sound the alarm. But communications in these remote areas are almost nonexistent and it will take the rebels and hour, or perhaps two, to react. By that time we will have potted as many coca plants as we can transport and we'll leave."

Gorman continued, "I'm sure the soldiers would love to stay and fight it out with the rebels, but that's not what they were trained to do. Hit and run is one of their specialties, and that's what they'll do today. I've encouraged the pilot to put on a little extra speed so maybe we can catch up."

A few minutes out of Bogota and they saw nothing below but green. There was an occasional dirt road and occasional dirt trail, but otherwise it was all green.

The helicopter droned on. An hour later the noise of the engine lessened and the pressure on their seats told them they were descending. And suddenly below, breaking the monotony of green was a field with two army vehicles and a truck and soldiers on the field looking upward. The pilot landed the helicopter deftly in the center of he field.

Gorman was on the ground almost before the helicopter was. He discussed the situation with Captain Valdez. Valdez had under his command a lieutenant, a sergeant, a corporal and thirty soldiers. Half of the Commandos were stationed on the perimeter of the field to protect against intruders, while the others awaited orders.

Gorman soon had the operation in motion. A large, covered van, rented for the occasion, was parked near the center of the coca field. While soldiers dug out plants and put them in pots, others cut plants off with their machetes and bundled them with twine. Arturo was in the truck, arranging pots in rows and piling bundles of cuttings on top. Emily roamed the field with Petie, encouraging the soldiers to cut only the healthiest plants.

Within an hour the operation was complete. All of the pots of transplants had been stored and cuttings were piled to the roof. The doors at the rear of the van were slammed shut and locked.

In the meantime soldiers spread straw over the field and sprinkled it with gasoline. Setting fire to the field would create the impression that this was just a routine raid. There would be no indication that plants or cuttings had been removed.

Shots rang out! The shots were answered by more shots. Rebels had been alerted and the commandos were responding.

"All right," Gorman said, "let's get out of here."

They scrambled into the helicopter and in seconds were airborne. The van had already moved off the field. One group of commandos covered the withdrawal of the other and they all safely exited the field. By now the field was a mass of flames and the rebels could not have pursued, even if they had the courage to do so.

Gorman beamed, "Operation a success!"

He continued, "I'd like to congratulate all of you, Emily and Petie and Arturo. You conducted yourselves in a professional manner, just as though you had been carrying out raids of this kind all of your lives."

No one wanted to hog the credit so they all just exchanged glances with one another and smiled.

"We should be back at the Embassy in an hour, just in time for lunch."

But Gorman spoke too soon. They didn't hear shots because of the noise of the helicopter engine and the beat of the rotor blades, but they were markedly aware of bullets ricocheting off the cabin. The pilot banked violently to the left and the ricocheting stopped. But smoke streamed from the engine compartment.

"We've been hit," the pilot stated, "my oil pressure is dropping. We're going to have to find a place to land."

"All right," Gorman said grimly, "but contact the Commandos. Tell them we're in bad trouble and give them the best directions as to where to find us."

The pilot sent a mayday message to the commandos. With smoke still streaming from the engine compartment the pilot followed a dirt trail that intersected with a dirt road. He descended and landed safely on the dirt road. They were about two hundred yards from the spot where the dirt trail intersected.

"Everybody out." Gorman ordered. "They saw us coming down and they'll be here in a few minutes looking for us. They'll be coming down that dirt trail. They'll look for us in the jungle near the helicopter, so were going to run back toward the trail. If we can cross it before they get here we'll hide there until the commandos arrive. Let's go."

They started to run toward the trail. Little Petie was lagging behind. Gorman stopped, picked her up and said, "Put our arms around my neck." Petie complied and Gorman resumed the race, outpacing the others with his pretty cargo.

As they approached the trail Gorman said, "Wait." He set Petie down on the ground and crept toward the trail. He had an automatic pistol, but what could one gun do against a band of rebel thugs?

Petie said, "Darn it, now I'll have to walk, just when I was getting used to being carried."

Gorman rushed back. "I can hear them coming. Their trucks can't be far down the trail. We'll have to stay where we are. Everyone, get down flat on the ground."

Everyone complied and within a minute two trucks came roaring down the trail, and with a screech of brakes turned right onto the dirt road. Both trucks were filled with rebel soldiers, some in uniform and some not. They were a decrepit ragtag bunch. All of them carried automatic weapons.

The vehicles came to a screeching stop when they reached the downed helicopter. As Gorman had predicted the rebels piled out of the truck and immediately started a search of the jungle nearby. Some of the rebels remained to guard the helicopter and checked the interior for passengers or loot.

"We'll just have to stay put here," Gorman said, "and hope the Commandos arrive before the rebels widen their search. I think we're only about ten miles from the coca field. It's been about three or four minutes since we advised them of our situation, so it should be about another three or four minutes before they get here." As the rebels widened their search, Gorman added, "I hope."

The rebels were approaching, nearer and nearer, pointing their weapons at every bush or hiding place, ready to shoot anyone on sight. The situation was becoming critical. Gorman hissed, "If it looks as though we are going to be discovered, I'll stand with my hands up and surrender. All of you stay down. That way we may be able to avoid being shot."

One of the rebels shouted, "Aqui." He had spotted something. Petie crept closer to Emily and Emily gave her hand a squeeze. "Sh!" she whispered.

At that moment, in the distance they heard the roar of truck engines, coming closer and becoming louder. It was the Commandos. One group of rebels panicked and ran for the jungle leaving their vehicle behind. The other group piled into their truck and raced away with one of the Commando trucks in pursuit.

Gorman rose and let out a warlike whoop. He ran toward the jungle after the fleeing rebels, firing his pistol as he ran.

"He obviously doesn't like rebels," Emily said.

Gorman kept firing until his pistol was empty, but the rebels were one hundred yards ahead of him and were running as he was. The odds against being hit were heavily in the rebels favor.

When Gorman returned Arturo asked, "How many did you get?"

"I lost count," Gorman grinned. "Let's go, people," he added.

As they approached the Commandos they saw that two of the rebels had been captured and sat dejectedly on the ground. Three has been shot dead as they tried to escape into the jungle.

The Commandos pushed the rebel truck a safe distance away from the helicopter and overturned it in the ditch beside the road. It was doused with gasoline and set on fire.

In the meantime the van with the potted plants and plant cuttings arrived. It had lagged behind the Commandos. The truck was being driven by an Embassy employee.

The pilot checked the damage to the helicopter. An oil line had been severed by a bullet. Oil had splashed onto the engine and that had caused the excessive smoke.

"I could repair it with masking tape," he said, "but it might let go somewhere between here and Bogota, and under less favorable conditions."

It was decided that they would radio for help. Minutes later the pilot reported another helicopter was on its way with a mechanic and parts.

The second Commando truck returned. The rebel truck they were chasing had overturned in the ditch about three miles down the road. The rebels abandoned the vehicle and ran for the jungle. Three rebels were shot dead. The truck was doused with gasoline and set on fire.

Gorman discussed the situation with Valdez, the Commando officer in charge, and with the pilot. With the loss of eight men and two trucks the rebels were undoubtedly disheartened and it was unlikely that they would regroup and return with reinforcements. But that was not a certainty. It would be at least an hour before the helicopter could be repaired.

It was decided that the two women would be evacuated in the truck with the plants, accompanied by one of the Commando units. The other unit would stand guard over the helicopter. Arturo and Gorman would remain behind and return with the pilot.

XVIII

As they approached the street to the Embassy two hours later, the Commandos peeled off and left. They did not stop to receive expressions of appreciation but, the occupants of the van waved their gratitude to their departing escort. The driver of the van made a left turn onto a side street.

Alarmed, Emily said, “Where are you taking us?”

“All deliveries and freight enter through the rear gate, Miss.”

Emily said, “Er . . yes, of course.”

The driver clicked on his opener and the gate opened. The helicopter had already landed and left, leaving Arturo and Gorman on the premises. They were obviously relieved to see that Emily and Petie, and the van and its contents had returned safely. The driver was intent on returning it to the rental agency, but he was to be pressed into service unloading the van.

Gorman led them to the far corner of the compound. "This area," he said, "has been reserved for your use."

"Now the hard work begins for us," Emily said. She referred to the unloading of the contents of the van.

A large picnic table had been set up and the cuttings, as they were removed from the van, were placed near it. Potted plants were placed in a separate area. Gorman worked along with the group.

"He certainly doesn't act like a diplomat," Petie observed.

"And he certainly doesn't act like the stuffy Mr. Quinn who met us at the airport," Emily added.

Gorman, sweating like a Trojan, was outpacing all of them in his work effort. And his smiling face said he was obviously enjoying it.

"This is a physical man," Emily said. Petie nodded.

There were ninety-six potted plants and Arturo took charge and saw that they were properly arranged and watered. The bundles of cuttings were stacked near the table. The freezer chest Emily had asked for had been set up in a storage room near the work area.

Now that the heavy work was done Gorman excused himself and left.

Emily, Petie and Arturo began stripping the leaves from the coca plants, one leaf at a time, and placed in plastic bags. As the bags were filled they were placed in the freezer chest.

Two hours later they had stripped only about one third of the plants. They were all tired after an eventful day.

Emily said, "We'd better knock it off for today. We'll finish the rest tomorrow."

The remaining plant cuttings were sprayed with water to keep them fresh and they were covered with a plastic tarp.

XIX

The next morning they started work at eight a.m. and by noon the last of the coca leaves had been stripped and bagged.

Petie looked at Emily and said, “You look beautiful, Emily.”

Emily, a little puzzled said, “Thank you Petie, but what brought that on?”

“It’s your face. You’re glowing, like a beautiful angel from heaven.”

“Wow!” Emily replied.

They had been out in the sun most of the previous day and today since early morning. Emily had developed a rosy glow to her cheeks and looked vibrantly healthy. Petie, with her black hair and her darker suntanned complexion was beginning to look like one of the natives.

Gorman came by and invited them to lunch in the kitchen.

Lunch over, Gorman said, "The Ambassador will be arriving here at about two. In the meantime feel free to prowl about and use any of the facilities; we have an exercise room, a billiard room, a music room and, of course, a library. There is also an outdoor pool beside the flower garden."

Emily looked at her soiled work clothes. "Perhaps we could run back to our hotel and change. I'd feel a little uncomfortable meeting an ambassador looking like this."

"Don't worry about it, Emily. The Ambassador is aware of the work you are carrying out and I'm sure he will understand."

Emily and Petie settled down in the library while Arturo investigated the other facilities.

Arturo returned and said, "Too bad we don't have our bathing suits. The pool is a beauty."

The Ambassador arrived promptly at two and came into the library to meet his guests. He was a man in his mid sixties, tall and slender with an upright bearing. He was a combination of reserved and cordial which made him well suited to the diplomatic service. He shook hands with all and inquired into the state of their health and their recent activities.

"Miss Smith," the Ambassador said, "while your friends are enjoying the library there are some things I would like to discuss with you." Emily rose. "Please come with me."

He had neatly dismissed Petie and Arturo without causing offense.

As the Ambassador was a combination of the reserved and the cordial, so his office was a combination of opulence and decorum. Richly paneled walls and beamed ceiling were complemented by thickly carpeted floors. Gilt-framed paintings decorated the walls.

"I apologize for my appearance, Sir," Emily said as she looked down at her soiled and rumpled work clothes.

"That's quite all right, Miss Smith. The work you are doing is of great importance, and in instances such as this, practicality triumphs over decorum."

The centerpiece of the office was a magnificent desk. Two grown adults could lie on it, head to head, with plenty of room left beyond their feet. The desk was of mahogany, rich in color and grain. It was curved like a half moon on the inside, where the user of the desk sat, and had one angular bend on the side opposite. The perimeter of the desktop was inlaid with hardwood veneers, a combination of triangles, squares, circles and random designs. The near side of the desk was flanked by six leather-upholstered arm chairs, arranged in such a fashion that all faced the user of the desk. The desktop was polished, so much that slight reflections of nearby objects were apparent.

Emily was intrigued. "I've never seen such a beautiful piece of furniture," she said, running her fingers lightly over the surface.

"Thank you," said the Ambassador. He was about to get to the business at hand when Emily added. "And the windows are magnificent."

Behind the desk were three arched windows, rising from near the floor. The center window reached almost to the ceiling, and the flanking windows were slightly lower. In the center of each window there was inlaid a rectangular panel of leaded glass.

"You are very observant, Miss Smith. Of all of the hundreds of people who visit this office in a year, not one ever appreciates its true beauty."

Emily was wide eyed. "Ambassador this . . . this is the most beautiful room I've ever seen."

The Ambassador was obviously pleased. "Thank you, Miss Smith, and may I add that I think you have an acute appreciation of the beautiful."

Looking down at the desk he continued, "I could spend an hour explaining the significance of each of the inlays on the desk. I've been in the diplomatic service since I graduated from college over forty years ago. Each one of the inlays represents a significant episode in my life. The desk has been with me for many years, and just recently I've had the inlays installed by a talented local artist."

Emily ran her fingers over the surface again.

"As for the windows, the leaded glass panels are again a self-anointed emolument. The panels on the left and right are the colors of the countries in which I have served. The colors, of course, being take from the colors in their national flags. And the colors in the center panel represent the colors of America, red, white and blue."

Emily was awestruck by the Ambassador's intense sincerity.

"The colors have such an inner glow," Emily observed.

"I've often wondered about that myself. I believe they must absorb some of the spectrum of the natural light from behind."

"The paintings you see on the walls," he led Emily to the paintings on he left, and continued, "depict the beginnings of America, from colonial days to through the Civil War."

"None of the paintings are expensive. They were the best I could afford at their time of purchase."

There were a dozen paintings on each wall. The first of the paintings depicted a woman making homespun cloth on a hand loom. Further on was a painting of Washington crossing the Delaware to raid Trenton. And still beyond that, Lincoln giving his address at Gettysburg. The Ambassador explained the significance of each scene. It was a pictorial review of American History.

Emily followed the Ambassador to the opposite wall.

"And here, from the end of the Civil War through the present."

There was Roosevelt at San Juan Hill, paintings of scenes from both World Wars, the astronauts on the moon. And again, the Ambassador described in detail each scene as it related to American History.

"All of the paintings I have collected over the years were by contemporary artists, none of them famous because of my financial limitations. And from all of this, Miss Smith, you may conclude that you have been briefly entertained by a vainglorious but patriotic American."

"I've never enjoyed a history lesson like this one."

"And now, Miss Smith, "let's get down to business."

Emily glanced at her watch. She had been here an hour. They were just now to talk about the pathogen program.

"You may have heard that the massacre in Los Angeles caused a sensation in Washington. It was realized that if your much under-funded operation received such drastic attention from the drug people then it must be causing them great concern. And if they were concerned they must believe that your pathogenic program could cause them great harm. The long and the short of it was that all of those concerned felt that the program should be greatly expanded."

"The operation here, of course, is only a pilot program and will be vastly expanded when suitable facilities can be found and proper security arranged. In the meantime, you will carry on as was previously arranged by Mr. Armitage."

Emily made no comment but nodded her understanding.

"There is just one more thing. You have been staying at a hotel. It would be preferable if you were to live here at the Embassy and you should move over today."

"Is there some kind of danger?" Emily asked.

"We don't think so, just a precaution."

The Ambassador buzzed his secretary. "Please ask Mr. Gorman to come in," he requested.

Gorman entered wearing a gray pinstripe suit. It seemed incompatible with his suntanned, freckled face. He gave Emily a questioning look.

"Miss Smith and her assistants will be moving into the Embassy, Edward. Please arrange for the proper accommodations. Also, have the limousine take them to their hotel and wait while they pack their clothing and personal things."

Excuse me sir," Gorman replied, "but the limousine is scheduled to pick up the three Congressmen at the airport, Quinn is just now getting ready to leave."

"Damn, I forgot about them. Congressmen always have to nose into anything that they can insert into their records. They are obviously interested in the pathogen program."

He continued, "All right, have Quinn drop off Miss Smith and her assistants at their hotel." He turned and said to Emily, "I'm afraid you will have to hire a taxi for your return trip."

"If the truth be known, Ambassdor," Emily quipped, "we are more accustomed to taxi cabs than we are to limousines."

The Ambassador chuckled and this puzzled Gorman. The Ambassador seldom chuckled. . .

The Ambassador accompanied them out of his office. He walked to the library and beckoned to Petie and Arturo. "Time to leave." He accompanied them to the entry of the Embassy. The limousine was waiting. The Ambassador shook hands with each in turn and said, "I will look forward to seeing all of you at dinner this evening."

Gorman walked down the steps with them. When he was out of earshot of the Ambassador he asked Emily, "What on earth happened in there? I was expecting that you'd be finished in there in ten minutes. You were in there for over an hour."

"We just got to talking," Emily replied.

The Ambassador was still standing on the landing in front of the entry. He waved as Emily got into the limousine.

XX

It took half an hour to pack. Arturo was waiting for them in the lobby. There was a taxi parked in front of the hotel. The driver loaded their luggage into the trunk and, following instructions, headed for the American Embassy.

When they stopped for the signal light at the 'T' intersection with the street leading to the Embassy a limousine with darkened windows pulled up to the left beside them. The taxi driver, with hands clenched tightly on the steering wheel, stole furtive glances at the limo.

The light changed and both vehicles started up and turned left toward the Embassy. The park with its iron railing was to their right. The taxi pulled to a stop at the entry to the park. The limousine pulled slightly ahead and swerved to the right to cut off any forward progress of the taxi. The taxi driver, seeing this, scrambled over into the front passenger seat, opened the door of the taxi and fled.

Two men emerged from the limousine, one a bulky unkempt ruffian and the other the man with the slouch hat, the same man Emily had seen in the hallway on the day of the massacre, and the same man they had seen speeding toward them in the arroyo.

Both of them brandished pistols. The unkempt one opened the taxi door and ordered them. "Out."

The three piled into the limousine followed by the two gunmen. The limousine sped away.

Emily, hiding her fear asked, "Who are you? Where are you taking us?"

Her questions elicited no response.

Emily took a deep breath and said, "I demand to know where we are being taken."

The man with the slouch hat turned, pointed his pistol at her head and answered, "Shut up."

That was the end of the conversation. They rode on in silence, and not without apprehension.

Emily reviewed the events in her mind. The Ambassador was obviously aware of some kind of danger. That was the purpose of having them move into the Embassy. One of the drug dealers had authorized the massacre in Los Angeles to get possession of one of the cassettes of pathogen. They had also killed all of the persons engaged in the production of the pathogen. Except me.

"But if they wanted to kill me, why didn't they just shoot me instead of kidnapping the three of us?"

The feeling of guilt was creeping up on Emily. Were Petie and Arturo now in danger because of her?

They were aware that there was more of the pathogen stored at the jungle location near Puerto Vallarta. The man with the slouch hat, who had now taken them prisoner, had obviously been in search of it. But they would have no way of knowing that it had been taken by Montoya.

Petie whispered to Emily, “Where do you think they’re taking us?”

“Shh! We’ll talk later. We don’t want to upset this thug.” Emily replied, referring their captor.

Emily continued with her thoughts. That must be it, they would be held for ransom, the ransom in this case being the cassette of pathogen. Yes but . . . there's always a 'yes but,' we no longer have the cassette and have no idea what Montoya may have done with it, or even where he might now be.

Petie moved closer to Emily, as if asking for protection. Emily put her arm around Petie’s shoulder and gave her a squeeze.

At least they had not been harmed, and the Embassy would have time to negotiate with them, whoever they are.

It was dark when the limousine pulled up in front of a wide iron gate. As the gate swung open an armed, uniformed guard stepped out from the shadows and waved the limousine through.

They drove down a paved driveway. From the glow of the headlights of the limousine they could see the outline of trees on each side. Farther on they could see the shadowy outline of a large building, probably residential from its appearance. The limousine passed around the side of the building and then onto a large, tiled courtyard, lighted by ornamental light standards. There were several soldiers standing guard, neatly uniformed and carrying automatic weapons.

The limousine stopped at a door at the rear of the building. They were directed down a passageway that led to a flight of stairs.

Petie whispered to Emily, "I smell food." Emily nodded in agreement, they must be in some kind of residential building. They could smell food; someone was preparing dinner.

The man with the slouch hat, waving his pistol, herded them up the stairs. They reached a long hallway with doors to the left and right. They were stopped at the first door to the right, the door was opened and, with a wave of the pistol Arturo was directed to enter. He complied and the door was closed and locked.

The procession continued and Emily and Petie were directed into the next room.

Petie put her arms around Emily's waist and her head on her shoulder and said, "Emily, tell me what's happening."

"I don't know for sure, Petie, but I think we're being held for ransom."

"But who would pay ransom for us? We're just ordinary people, not rich or anything."

"I may be wrong, Petie, but I think the ransom they're after is the cassette that we went to Puerto Vallarta to pick up."

"But we don't have the cassette, Montoya has it."

"They don't know that, Petie, and as long as they think we still have it I think we're safe."

They were in a large bedroom, carpeted and comfortably furnished. There was a bathroom adjoining. The barred windows in the bedroom overlooked the courtyard. Outside they could see soldiers, heavily armed, patrolling the area. The building at the back of the courtyard was obviously a barracks building for the soldiers. Without meaning to peek, Emily and Petie looking down from their second floor bedroom could see, through slots in the window blinds, men in their underwear and other scanty attire.

"I can't even imagine how we could escape from here, Petie."

Petie walked over the wall between the two bedrooms. She tapped on it three times. Moments later there were three responding taps.

"Do you know Morse code Emily?"

"No, and I'm sure Arturo doesn't know it either."

"It would be nice if we could send a message to him."

"What message would you send?"

"I'd just ask him if he was OK."

"You just saw him less than five minutes ago."

"Yes, but I miss him. We've been together so much. And you said yourself that we're a team."

Emily put her arms around Petie. "We *are* a team, Petie. And we'll get out of this together. All we can do now is keep our composure and see what happens next."

What happened next was the sound of the bedroom door being unlocked. The door swung open and a uniformed guard entered. He stood aside and a maid pushed in a cart. Dinner was being served.

Dinner consisted of soup, roast chicken with vegetables, and fruit for dessert. Coffee in a large silver pot accompanied the meal.

When the guard and maid had withdrawn Emily said, "It looks delicious, Petie. Let's dig in."

"Maybe this is our last meal," Petie giggled.

Dinner over, Emily and Petie tried to relax.

"I wish I had something to read," Emily said. "When I worked the mountains in Los Angeles County I spent many hours at night reading. Mr. Andrews had an extensive library. Reading became a habit and I missed it when I returned to civilization."

Half an hour later the door was unlocked and the maid, accompanied by the guard, wheeled the cart out of the room.

As she was leaving Petie rushed over to her and with a smile said, "Thank you, the food was delicious."

The maid probably didn't understand what Petie said, but she knew it was a message of appreciation, and she responded with a smile of her own.

XXI

In the morning, after a night of fitful sleep, Emily and Petie showered, put on yesterday's clothes and amused themselves by looking out of the bedroom window. A sergeant was instructing soldiers on the use of automatic weapons. Probably new recruits.

"Whoever our host is, he has his own personal army," Emily commented. “Just from up here we've seen thirty or forty of them, and most of them have automatic weapons."

Petie was more interested in the soldiers. "I don't think I've ever seen so many nice looking men in one place at one time. Do you feel guilty about peeking at them through their windows last night?"

"No, I don't, Petie. And if we're still here tonight, I'll blindfold you so you won't feel guilty either."

"Emily!" Petie cried indignantly, "I don't think it would be necessary to go to that extreme!"

They were attracted by the sound of the door being unlocked. This time a different maid, accompanied by a different guard, wheeled in their breakfast: bacon and eggs with sliced tomatoes, and thick slices of toasted bread. And, of course, a pot of Colombian coffee.
As they were eating Petie said, "If they keep this up they're going to ruin my figure."

Emily, looking at Petie's trim lines said, "Don't worry, Petie, it will take them quite a while to do that."

Waiting was what bothered Emily most. They had been here fourteen or sixteen hours and nothing had happened. They had spoken to no one. Looking at her watch she noted it was almost nine o'clock.

The door of the room was being unlocked. Two armed guards were in the hallway and motioned for them to come out. In the hallway they opened the door to the next room and Arturo emerged. They all exchanged smiles.

Petie was about to rush forward to give Arturo a hug. Emily grasped her by the arm and said, "Not now, Petie."

They descended by the same back stairway. Off the hallway on the main floor were several doors. One door was opened for them and they were ushered into a large room with beamed ceiling and carpeted floors. Bookcases lined the walls and the room was furnished with leather upholstered chairs and reading tables.

"This is just like a real library," Petie said.

Arturo investigated, checking titles on row after row of books. He returned to Emily and Petie, seated comfortably in the upholstered chairs. Petie had her feet up on an adjoining chair and gave the impression that she didn't have a care in the world.

Arturo reported, "Most of the books deal with the history of South America and the history of Colombia, and that sort of thing."

"Any famous authors?" Emily asked.

"The only one I recognized was Borges, but I'm not up much on South American authors."

Arturo continued, "But what's scary is that he has dozens of books about the life and accomplishments of Joseph Stalin, and even a few about Adolph Hitler, including Hitler's *Mein Kampf.*"

"From what I've read, Arturo, many parts of South America were a haven for Nazis after the collapse of Germany in World War II. It's quite likely that literature in sympathy with the Nazis may have infiltrated into Colombia. But if our host is a Joseph Stalin fan, I'd say that *is* scary."

Petie piped up, "Are there any American authors?"

"Only a few, Hemingway, Steinbeck, and someone named Paul Theroux. It's surprising how America, as great as she is, produced so few outstanding writers."

At one end of the library was a life-sized painting of a man, without a crown, but clad in regal robes. He was a large man, seated in a large, high-backed arm chair. His head was held high, too high, and it gave him the look of superior haughtiness. But though his head was held high, he looked down on the viewer with disdain. There were three steps up to a platform on which the high-backed arm chair stood.

"Do you think that could be our host?" Emily asked.

"I hope not, Petie said, "he looks like an evil man."

"It seems scary," Arturo added, "he has a strange look, as though he thought he were a king, or even worse, as though he were God himself."

"If he's a fan of Joseph Stalin or Adolph Hitler, then we're in bad trouble." Emily added.

The door of the library opened. A tall, thin, elderly man in a dark-blue business suit entered. He said, "Mr. Rodriguez will see you now, please follow me."

Emily caught up with the man and asked, "Who is Mr. Rodriguez?"

"He is your host," was the reply.

Across the hallway from the library they entered another room, much like the library room, but there was no furniture, just bare tiled floors and bare painted walls. At one end of the room was a stage-like platform, with access by three wide steps.

On the stage, in an enormous, high-backed arm chair, sat an enormous man. He was obviously the man in the painting in the library, but was much greater in size. His great bulk filled the chair.

His face was a balloon accompanied by symmetrical bulges of fat beneath his eyes, on his cheeks and jowls. Even his forehead was overlain with bulges of fat. His head was bald and shiny and only tufts of graying hair separated his head from his ears.

Framed in fat, his eyes were two beady apertures in his intemperate face.

So fat were his shoulders that he appeared to have no neck, just a head on top of a body. He wore a loose short-sleeved shirt. Fat bulged from his forearms and sagged over the arms of his arm chair.

He wore what might best be described as pantaloons, that hid his obesity below his waist. But in plain view the fat on his chest sagged down onto his belly, and the fat of his belly sagged down onto his lap, like a balloon, ready to burst. But this was the man who was in the painting, the man in the regal robes. He was much more obese than the man in the painting, but there was no doubt that it was the same man.

Emily and Petie and Arturo were led before him. All of them immediately recognized one of the men who stood behind him and to his left. It was the evil man in the limousine who had taken them prisoner.

"My name is Felix Rodriguez," the fat man said. "I am your host. And thank you, Miss Smith, for paying me this visit."

Thoughts rushed through Emily's mind, "Who is this

man, and how does he know my name?" But she calmed herself and replied, "Thank you for the invitation."

Rodriguez greeting was meant to intimidate. At first he was taken aback by Emily's response. But then he leaned back and let out a roar of laughter that reverberated through the hollow room.

"I'm glad to see you have a sense of humor, Miss Smith. The man you see standing to my left has no sense of humor at all."

He waved a fat hand to his left. The man to his left was the man with the slouch hat, but now as he stood there he was without a hat and without his dark glasses. His black hair was slicked down. His eyes were like black holes, without life and without expression.

“You have met him before, Miss Smith, but you have never been introduced. This is Juan de Jesus.”

It came to Emily like a flash of light. This was the ‘Wanda’ that she thought Sheldon’s words referred to.
But he wasn’t saying ‘Wanda,’ he was trying to say ‘Juan’ and pronounced only the ‘d’ of his second name before he collapsed and died. So, in addition to the five victims in the office, de Jesus had shot and killed Sheldon as well.

“He was very angry with you,” Rodriguez continued. “He almost drowned in the arroyo at Puerto Vallarta. When the rain started and the arroyo flooded he and his friend had to scramble up out of the arroyo. They clung to the undergrowth for over an hour before the flood water subsided. Their Jeep was washed down the arroyo. When the flood was over they found it a mile down the arroyo. It had turned over onto its side and had rolled over, probably a hundred times. Needless to say, it was a total wreck."

"Fortunately de Jesus had accomplices waiting for him on the beach in another vehicle. When the rush of water had subsided they drove up the wash and picked up de Jesus and his friend."

"Just as Montoya had predicted." Emily thought.

"I tell you this only because de Jesus is a sensitive person and you have caused him some embarrassment. He can be impetuous at times, the killings in Los Angeles are a good example. It would have been better, all round, if he had not shot all of those people. But he was irritated because he did not find the descriptive matter regarding the disbursement of the pathogens."

"Impetuous!" Emily thought. "He killed five unarmed persons, and Rodriguez refers to him as impetuous!"

Rodriguez continued. "Please be considerate of his feelings, Miss Smith, he will be supervising your activities and we wouldn't want any undue amount of friction to develop between you."

"I don't know what your reference to our activities means. Why have we been brought here?"

"I'm sure by now, Miss Smith, you must be aware that we have had an insight into your operation for some time, and still do. It was our intention to destroy all of the pathogen you had produced when the time was right. We were aware that you had limited funding and the destruction of the pathogens would bring your operation to a halt. Any further funding would be denied and your assault on our industry would end."

"Then along came Montoya, the wild card. He stole from you the pathogen that de Jesus was to have acquired. He hates Montoya too, but then de Jesus hates so many people, this was just one more to be added to his list."

Rodriguez recognized the ironic humor in his statement and chuckled, but because of his great bulk the chuckle came forth like a series of guttural guffaws.

"Montoya is a very enterprising man. He convinced me that instead of destroying the pathogen I should use it to trample my competition. You may not be aware of it, Miss Smith, but I am the most powerful drug dealer in South America; perhaps the most powerful in the whole world."

"I have dispatched Montoya to Bolivia with the pathogen. He doesn't have the instructions on how to disburse it into the coca fields, but he said he had read the instructions and knew the procedures. He wanted five million U. S. dollars as payment for the destruction of the coca fields in Bolivia. Of course, that was ridiculous. We agreed on one million. In the meantime

I've given him one-hundred thousand dollars start up money. He said he would have the project underway in two or three weeks. And if he does a good job, *maybe* I'll give him five-hundred thousand."

Rodriguez, amused by his own duplicity, filled the room with another roar of laughter.

Emily was about to inform Rodriguez that Montoya did, in fact, have the written instructions. He had stolen them from her hotel room. But then she recalled the admonition of Armitage, 'Do not volunteer any information that you have not been asked for.'

Rodriguez continued. "The plan that has now evolved is this: If Montoya is successful in Bolivia he will move his operation into Peru and carry out the same work there. In the meantime, I will wipe out some of the coca fields here so that dealers will be aware that they will have to deal through me, or perish."

"Aren't you afraid," Emily asked, " that you will start an epidemic and destroy the coca fields in Colombia?"

"Oh no. I'll just destroy a few fields in outlying areas. The dealers are good businessmen. They will get the message."

"And that is where you and your friends come in, Miss Smith. We have a secluded retreat up in the mountains, not too far from here. We will need a continual supply of the pathogen you have produced in order to carry out our plans. You will create a laboratory there. As long as we have your cooperation you will be well treated."

"With your help, Miss Smith, I will become the most powerful and the wealthiest man in the world. I'll make your 'Bill Gates' look like a pauper." Amused by his own wit, Rodriguez let out another roar of laughter.

"This is such an important project I would like to accompany you to the laboratory site, but I have to attend a luncheon. As a matter of fact I will be the guest of honor. You may find it disconcerting because of your American prejudice, but here in my part of the world I am a public benefactor. I provide employment for my people, and a standard of living far higher than anywhere else in Colombia."

"De Jesus will accompany you to the retreat. He knows the rules; so long as you cooperate you have nothing to fear."

Emily took a deep breath and, drawing on her reserve of courage said, "I would appreciate it, Sir, if you would direct Mr. de Jesus to refrain from pointing his pistol at me, or my friends, unless, of course, he is intending to shoot us."

Rodriguez again roared with laughter. "Did you hear that, Juan, the lady objects to your unchivalrous conduct."

"All right, Miss Smith, de Jesus will conduct himself with proper restraint."

During the proceedings de Jesus had been staring fixedly ahead, as though he had no interest in the discussion. But now he turned his head and looked down at Emily from the platform, with obvious hatred in his evil, black eyes.

XXII

A van was parked near the rear door through which they had entered the building the previous evening. They climbed in and were seated. De Jesus and a driver climbed into the van and they sped around to the front of the building. At night it had looked large and looming, but in daylight it was an impressive palace. It was soon out of sight as they sped down a smoothly paved, tree-lined driveway and through the gated entry onto a paved highway.

Within a few miles the paved highway turned into gravel.

Petie whispered to Emily, “Do you have any idea where we’re going?”

“Only that we seem to be going north and east.”

The van sped on. The gravel road was relatively smooth, with occasional stretches of corrugated wash-board that shook the van and its passengers unmercifully. She wanted to ask de Jesus where they were going, but after the malice he had silently directed at her in the meeting with Rodriguez, she refrained.

The van rattled on and they were now in a broad valley with mountains to their right and higher mountains to their left. The van slowed down and turned left off the highway onto a dirt road. Emily looked at her watch. They had been traveling north and easterly for forty-five minutes. They were now headed straight for the mountain ahead, but the ascent was obviously too steep for any vehicle to attempt.

In a few minutes they turned left started a gentle climb. Then they turned right and continued on an upward incline. They were on a series of switchbacks that would eventually take them to their destination, wherever that might be. Each switchback followed the next, back and forth. They were heading southerly when the incline became much steeper; the road narrowed. It would be difficult for vehicles to pass one another.

The steepness of the grade caused the driver to shift into low gear as the van ground its way upward. Ahead all that could be seen was blue sky. Emily looked to her right and saw they were precariously close to the edge of the road. If the van should tumble off the road it would continue to roll until it reached the bottom of the mountain three thousand feet below.

At this point the driver made a hairpin turn to the left. They were on an outcropping of rock and were turning directly away from the dangerous edge of the road. Now they curved off to their right and again followed the incline of the mountain face. The road had widened, but the rocky, uneven surface sent violent shudders through the van. In the tumult within the van passengers clung to anything that would help lessen the shock.

De Jesus screamed at the driver, "Slow down, you fool, are you trying to kill us?"

The driver slowed down to less than half speed, but

still the rocky surface transferred shock to both to the van and to the passengers.

Two more switchbacks and they were on level ground. Ahead were trees and shrubbery and beyond an open plateau.

Passing through the trees the prisoners beheld a beautiful mansion, a mansion with tiled roof and white stucco walls and Spanish endearments to doors and windows. It was a two story building with four steps up to a porch and entry at the front. The roofs of the porch and entry were tiled to match the roof of the main building.

There was a two car attached garage on the near side of the mansion and a paved driveway leading to it. The pavement wrapped around to the front of the building. The garage had white stucco walls and tile roof to match the mansion, but was without adornments and appeared to be of more recent construction than the main building. It didn't look to be much in use. There were weeds growing at the sides of the driveway and grass had sprouted in the cracks in the concrete surface. There was a Toyota pickup truck parked on the driveway, but nearer to the front entry of the mansion.

In the background the mountains continued their ascent and provided an exquisite setting for the building.

The van stopped on the paved surface in front of the mansion; with a wave of his pistol de Jesus indicated that they should get out. Despite their unknown and foreboding future the prisoners were all much relieved to be out of the van.

A man came out onto the front deck and then stumped down the stairs. He limped over to speak to de Jesus. What was different about him was that he wasn't waving a pistol in his hand. He pointed to the far side of the building and de Jesus, following his directive, indicated to the prisoners that they should proceed in that direction.

The three of them followed the unspoken instruction and walked ahead, followed by de Jesus, the driver of the van, and the man with the limp. This was the first time they had a good look at the driver; they had seen him from behind and noted that he had greasy, black, unkempt hair; now they saw he had squinty yellow-brown eyes and the pasty skin on his face hung in folds, as though he had at one time been overly obese and had more recently lost much weight. When his colorless lips parted they revealed broken, yellowed teeth.

Petie looked at him and shuddered.

Beyond the corner of the house was a small guest house, with tiled roof and white stucco walls, similar in design but obviously newer than the main building. Inside the building consisted of a large room which doubled as a living room and bedroom. To one side was a bathroom and an open kitchen. It looked as though someone had been using the room for sleeping quarters. There were articles of clothing strewn about and the room gave the general appearance of untidiness. This was probably where the man with the limp slept. The kitchen didn't look much used so he probably took his meals in the main building.

Emily whispered to Petie, "We're going to have to find a way out of here right away before they get organized. Otherwise we might be here forever."

"Or until they kill us," Petie added.

De Jesus said, "This is where you will set up your laboratory. You will give me a list of the equipment you will need and Mr. Rodriguez will obtain it for you." He had the pathogen cassette in his hand.

Emily put her shoulders back, raised her nose in the air, and with the snootiest expression she could muster said, "This is totally unsatisfactory. All of this filthy carpeting and furniture will have to be removed, the place will have to be sanitized and all of the equipment in the kitchen will have to be discarded. The windows will have to be sealed as well as the doors."

Emily was doing her best to work herself up into a tantrum.

"I refuse to do anything until I discuss this personally with Mr. Rodriguez." She almost screamed it at de Jesus.

"Mr. Rodriguez," said de Jesus, trying to placate her, "instructed that you would make an inventory of everything that you will need and I will return it to him, and he will get for you everything that you need."

Emily repeated, "I refuse to do anything until I discuss this personally with Mr. Rodriguez."

De Jesus raised his pistol, he used it as a gesture, almost as though it were a part of his right hand. The muzzle of the gun was touching Emily's throat.

"Go ahead," Emily said, "shoot me. I'm sure Mr. Rodriguez would be very pleased."

De Jesus didn't remove the gun. He just stared at Emily with his empty, evil, black eyes.

"When Mr. Rodriguez is finished with you," de Jesus said, lowering the gun, "We'll have a little party, you and I and your two friends. For entertainment I'll shoot each one of you, but not dead. I'll shoot one in the arm, one in the leg and maybe one in the foot. Then we'll have another round of shooting. This time I'll shoot one in the shoulder and one in the ribs, and one in the stomach. I might even put my gun in your mouth, Miss Smith, and blow a hole in one of your pretty cheeks. And I'll keep on shooting, and the three of you can sit around and watch one another bleed to death. Won't that be fun?"

Petie was terrified. Arturo just stood there with his mouth open and gaped.

"You're a madman!" Emily gasped.

De Jesus waved his pistol at them and, addressing the man with the limp said, "Take them to the house and lock them in the bedroom." He handed the cassette to the man with the limp and said, "Put this in the refrigerator." He put his gun in its holster and strode off.

The man with the limp said, "This way," and indicated a pathway which led from the guest house to the rear of the main building. He was the only one they had seen yet who didn't wear a pistol as part of his hand.

A pathway led behind the mansion with the mountain slope to the left. They came to a paved area behind the attached garage. There were a few garden tools and a propane gas cylinder next to the garage wall. There was a door leading to the inside of the garage.

There were no vehicles in the garage and it gave the appearance of being not much used. There was a water heater in the corner next to the rear wall, and a washer and dryer beside it. Three steps up provided entry to the door leading to the kitchen. Beyond the steps was a work bench with various tools and equipment.

The man with the limp went stiffly ahead into the kitchen, followed by Petie and Arturo. He placed the cassette in the freezer compartment, and then, turning to the ugly one who had followed said, "Take them to the bedroom." The ugly one waived them ahead with his pistol and he, and the man with the limp followed behind.

XXIII

They entered a vast living room area, a magnificent room with vaulted ceiling supported by massive, heavily-carved beams. The floors throughout were of reddish-brown Spanish tile covered here and there with rugs and carpet runners. On the rear wall, opposite the front entry was a wide and open stairway rising to a landing. From the landing, stairs to left and right led to balconies overlooking the living room. The balcony on the right followed the rear wall and then turned right again to provide access to two of the second floor bedrooms. As they entered their heels were clicking on the tiled floors.

The ugly one led the way and they all followed him, heels still clicking on he Spanish tile, Emily first, then Arturo followed by Petie. The man with the limp stopped at the bottom of the stairway, apparently not wanting to make the climb. When the ugly one reached the landing he stopped and waved his pistol indicating that they should turn to the right. Emily leading the way followed the turn in the balcony. On her left she saw an open bedroom door and started to enter it.

The ugly one shouted, "*No!*"

Emily backed out of the room and the ugly one reached in and closed the door. He then herded them into the next room adjoining.

Suddenly Petie began to scream. The ugly one had grasped her wrist and was trying to drag her from the room. While Petie continued to scream Emily rushed forward and grabbed her around the waist and pulled her back.

"You dirty son of a bitch," Emily screamed venomously at the ugly one, "let her go!"

He didn't know much English, but he knew what 'son of a bitch' meant. He raised his gun and pointed it at Emily, within three inches of her face.

Arturo advanced; with eyes blazing he shouted, "Rodriguez will *kill* you."

His words were like an electric shock down the spine of the ugly one. With Petie still screaming and, realizing what he had done, he released the grasp on her wrist; his gun hand dropped to his side and he stood rigidly still. His face and neck turned red under his mottled skin; he started to sweat.

The man with the limp entered the room, this time with gun in hand. "Que paso?" he demanded.

In a torrent of Spanish, Arturo described what had taken place. And in a torrent of Spanish, the man with the limp dismissed the ugly one from the room. His heels clicked his departure on the, tile floor. Without saying anything the man with the limp backed out of the room and closed the door. They heard a dead bolt slide into locked position.

Petie had her head buried on Emily's shoulder and was

still sobbing. Arturo stepped over, placed his hand on her shoulder and said, “Don’t worry little one, we won’t let any thing happen to you.”

Emily dabbed the tears from Petie's eyes with a soggy Kleenex; she stopped crying.

The room was large but sparsely furnished. There was a Spanish-style bed with massive legs and headboard and a chest of drawers to match. A large full length mirror on one wall and two carpet runners completed the furnishings.

There were iron bars outside of the casement windows. As they looked out Petie said, “My, what a lovely view!”

“Petie, you’re priceless!” Emily said as she tousled Petie’s glossy, black hair. To Arturo she said, “Two minutes ago she was in imminent danger of being raped, and I was in imminent danger of having my head blown off, we’re all prisoners and Petie is admiring the view.”

But to Petie she said more compassionately, “You’re right, Petie, it is a lovely view." From their vantage point they could see down into the valley below with green mountains in the background and the high, blue sky above. Emily continued, "And maybe when this is all over and Rodriguez is in jail, we’ll come back here and have a picnic." Petie smiled.

Despite her cheerful words, Emily realized they were in grave danger.

Despite her cheerful words, Emily realized they were in grave danger.

Parked on the driveway below was the Toyota truck.

Arturo walked over to the bed, took off his shoes and hopped up onto the mattress. He turned around and let his body fall full length onto the mattress. He lay there with his arms stretched out at his sides. “This is a great bed!” he said, and then looking slyly at Emily said, “do you think it’s big enough for the three of us?”

“Arturo,” Emily replied, “if we have to spend the night here, you’ll be sleeping on the floor. Now get up. We have to figure some way to get out of here.” Emily was about to say, “We’re in worse trouble than I thought,” but focused her attention on Arturo instead.

Arturo brought his knees up to his chin, bent his legs and rolled his body backward. Then, unrolling his body and shooting his legs forward, he catapulted his way into a standing position. Then he hopped lightly from the bed onto the floor.

“You’re very lithe.” Emily observed and then continued. “We have about two hours before de Jesus returns with Rodriguez.”

Arturo walked over to the door. "This door is hinged on the inside. If we could remove pins from the hinges we could slide the door open."

This was a heavy wooden door, and was heavily carved and was supported by three hinges.

"That's no good," Emily said, "the balcony outside looks down on the living room. If they didn't hear us remove the door they'd see us."

"Anyway." Arturo said dejectedly, "the center hinge has a cap welded to it so the pin can't be removed."

Emily looked at the hinge, and saw there was a small piece of metal that blocked the removal of the pin. She looked at the barred windows and observed, "This room must have been used as a prison cell."

Petie piped up, "Maybe this where they kept their enemies before they tortured them to death."

Emily shook her head. Despite the predicament they were in Petie was back to being her bright, cheerful self.

Emily went back to the window, reached out and tested the bars. They didn't move, not even a fraction of an inch.

Arturo, beside her said, "Even if we could get through the bars it's a long drop onto the pavement. We'd probably break our legs."

Petie inquired, "Couldn't we rip up the bed sheets and make a rope, the way they do in the movies, in prison breaks?"

Emily tried not to give Arturo a direct order as it seemed to grate against his macho, so she posed the question, "I wonder what's in the bathroom?"

Arturo replied, "I'll look."

He came back a minute later and reported, "There's a small window, high up. Petie could probably get through it, and if we could do the bed sheet thing she could get to the ground, and to the Toyota truck. But if the keys aren't in the truck, and they probably aren't, she would have to try to walk out of here, which would be almost impossible."

He was carrying a box of Kleenex which he handed to Emily. She and Petie both removed a small supply.

"No," Emily said, "We're all in this together and we'll all leave together."

Looking out of the window Emily said, "Arturo, the front of the garage is only about ten feet from where we're standing. That means it's directly below the next bedroom, the one we passed before we were herded in here. If we could get through the wall at the head of the bed, we could climb out onto the garage roof and then climb down to the back of the garage and make our way to the truck."

"Aren't the windows in there barred too?" Arturo asked.

"No. Don't you remember when we came up here I turned into that bedroom, I thought that's where we were being taken. Then the ugly one stopped me. But I was in the room and I know the windows were not barred. The room is smaller than this one. The furniture is the same, with the bed back to back with this one. But there's still one question. If the ignition key isn't in the truck, would you be able to start it?"

"Of course, I own a Toyota truck. I've started my truck before without a key, all I need is a knife, and maybe a screwdriver."

"There's a workbench in the garage. I'm sure we could find whatever you need there. Now, how about this wall?"

Arturo produced a hotel room key from his pocket. Rodriguez men had relieved them of their wallets, pocket books and cash, but somehow Arturo had retained his key.

"These are plastered walls. It will depend on how thick the plaster is and what kind of backing there is behind the plaster."

He took his key and scraped away at the wall near the floor and beside the bed. Within a few minutes he reported.

"The plaster is only about an eighth of an inch thick. It's very hard. but there's a wallboard backing behind it, probably gypsum, and by comparison it's quite soft. But it will take me hours to get through it with this key, even if my fingers hold out that long."

"I'll see if I can find something," Emily said.

She looked around the room, nothing. She went into the bathroom and came back a few minutes later carrying a metal rod about a foot long and an eight of an inch in thickness.

"The rod from the toilet float," She explained.

"Perfect!" Arturo said. It really wasn't perfect, in fact, as a tool it was less than functional but it was better than his hotel key; it would have to do. He tried to bend one end to make a handle but the rod wouldn't bend.

"Before we start on this we had better make sure one of us can slide under the bed." Emily said. "There's a bed the same as this one in there, and it's right next to this wall." She tapped on the wall next to the bed.

Emily turned to Petie. "Petie, you're elected, see if you can fit under this bed."

"Face down on the floor," Emily instructed. With Petie on the floor Emily pushed on her shoulder and hip till she slid under the bed. On her knees and looking at the space between Petie and the underside of the bed, Emily said, "She has more than an inch to spare."

Emily dragged Petie from under the bed, lifted her up and dusted her off.

"Thank you Petie, now sit down by the door and listen for anyone coming up the stairs." Petie complied, sitting on the floor with her back to the door and her legs stretched out and her ear to the crack between the door and the door frame.

Arturo and Emily dragged the bed away from the wall. Arturo started scraping the plaster at about the center of where the bed had been and about a foot above the floor. Little by little he extended a horizontal groove in the wall more than a foot wide. To satisfy himself as to the structure of the wall he punched a hole through the softer wallboard backing and inserted the rod. He pushed it forward till it stopped. He tapped on the back of the wall in the adjoining bedroom. . .

He turned his head and looked up to Emily's anxious eyes, "This is going to work, Emily, there's another wall like this one on the other side. But I have to stop for a rest, my hand is hurting."

Arturo had been scraping for almost an hour with the crude tool. Arturo held up his right hand, the one that was required to do all of the work. It wasn't bleeding, but it was pink and puffy and was obviously causing him distress.

Just then Petie said, "Someone is coming; it's the man with the limp." Petie could tell who it was by the uneven 'click-pause-click,' of his heels.

Emily and Arturo pushed the bed back into place. Arturo sat on the floor under the window with his legs outstretched. Emily and Petie sat primly on the bed. Looking at Arturo, Emily saw that there was white powder on his hands from the plaster wall. She wanted to signal to him but the door was already opening.

The man with the limp looked from one to another of them. Noticing the powder on Arturo's hands he said, "What's that on your hands?"

Arturo looked at his hands. He paused, then said, "There was some kind of white powder on the floor of the van. I must have got some on my hands."

"Why don't you wash them?"

"Good idea." Arturo jumped up and headed for the bathroom.

The man with the limp looked again at the women. Then he backed out of the room and the door closed; the dead bolt clicked.

XXIV

"It's just about an hour since we were locked up here. I guess he intends to check every hour to make sure we haven't escaped."

"And you notice," Arturo added, that he came up here himself. His limp makes it difficult for him to climb stairs, but obviously he doesn't trust the ugly one."

In the bathroom Arturo was running cold water on his puffy right hand. He took a hand towel from a rack and dried it. "It feels a little better," he said.

"It's too bad we don't have something to put on it." Emily looked in the medicine cabinet but it was empty. "Let's see if we can put some kind of handle on the rod, that might help."

"I tried," Arturo said, "but I couldn't bend it."

Emily went into the bedroom and groped under the bed till she found the rod. She returned to the bathroom.

"We'll jamb the rod between the door and the frame with about three inches for a handle. I'll push on the door from the inside and you try to bend it. That should give you enough leverage."

With the rod in place Emily leaned heavily on the door on the inside. On the outside Arturo grasped the rod and bent it without difficulty.

"Very clever, Miss Smith!"

"There isn't anything Emily can't fix," Petie chimed in.

"Just a minute." Emily tore a strip from the towel, wet it and wrapped it around the handle end.

Arturo tried out the new tool. “Petie’s right, Emily, you’re a genius.”

“Thank you Arturo, and you’re obviously an astute judge of character.” Emily rewarded him with one of her most charming smiles. And she added, “Let’s get back to work.”

Petie returned to her post at the door. Emily and Arturo slid the bed out from the wall. Arturo was able to work much more efficiently with the improved tool. With the horizontal and vertical channels completed, Arturo pried with his hand tool and the section he had been working on fell loose. He could now see the backside of the adjoining bedroom wall. Soon, with the new tool, he had completed the horizontal and vertical trenches in the backside of the wall.

"I could punch it through right now Emily."

"Wait a minute. We have to make sure no one comes back while we're trying to escape. If we can get one of them up here on some pretext . . . that's it, we'll tell him we need some food. You have better knuckles than I do, Arturo, start knocking on the door. Petie come and sit on the bed with me."

Arturo rapped as hard as he could intermittently for about thirty seconds. A minute later they could hear the man with the limp coming down the hall.

He opened the door. "What is it?" he demanded.

Arturo said, "We're very hungry. We haven't had anything to eat since early this morning. Could we have some food?"

The man with the limp said nothing but backed out of the room and locked the door.

"We're running short of time, Emily said, "we'll give him ten minutes. If he doesn't come back by then we'll have to assume we aren't getting any food and get moving out of here."

Petie sat by the door. Five minutes later she said, "I can hear him coming."

The door opened and the man handed Arturo a plate of warm tortillas with slices of cheese; there was a plastic glass on top.

"Get water from the bathroom," he said. And he backed out, closed the door and locked it.

Emily got water from the bathroom and they feasted on cheese wrapped in tortillas, with sips of water in between. They were all very hungry.

"All of us had better have a good drink of water. Once we're out of here it may be a long time before we get more."

The three of them went to the bathroom and each had a long drink. Arturo was looking closely at Petie. "Love in bloom," Emily thought.

Lying flat on the floor Arturo quietly punched out the rectangle of wallboard that he had worked on so diligently. Before him he saw the underside of the bed, and to the left, the tiled floor of the bedroom, and beyond that the door leading to the second floor hallway.

“We've done it!" he cried, " I can see the bedroom door from here”

Emily said, “OK Petie, front and center. Lie down on the floor, face down.”

Petie, shoes off, complied and eased her head and shoulders through the opening. She reached ahead pulling on the floor with the flat of her hands while Arturo pushed on her two tiny feet. Her shoulders passed through the opening, then her slender hips, and she was completely through.

Reaching through the opening Arturo continued to push on Petie’s feet while she struggled forward. Then Petie was free. She was standing. Arturo saw her feet and ankles heading toward the door. The door opened, the feet and ankles disappeared and the door closed. . .

"Petie made it!" Arturo cried.

"Quick, Arturo, push the bed into place," Emily directed.

Petie unlatched their prison door from the outside and entered. She quickly and quietly closed the door behind her. "They're watching a soccer game on TV."

"Down here they call it football," Arturo noted.

Emily gave her a hug, "Great work, Petie!"

Arturo said, "I'd like to give you a hug too, Petie, but my Latin upbringing won't permit it."

"But my American upbringing will," Petie said. She gave him a hug and a kiss on the cheek.

Arturo smiled, he was obviously pleased but under his dark skin he blushed.

"Petie, will you quit fooling around," Emily said.

"I'm sorry Emily."

"We'll have to be careful. They can see up here from the living room."

Emily opened the door a crack. Down below the two men, the man with the limp and the ugly one, were watching television. A good thing the TV was on the far wall of the living room so the men were facing away from the second-floor prison room.

"All right," said Emily, "take off your shoes Arturo. We'll have to sneak into the next room; Petie first, then you, Arturo, and I'll close the door and follow."

Emily opened the door a crack. There was a roar from the television set. The two men hunched forward. There was a crucial play in the game they were watching.

"Now," Emily hissed. Petie and Arturo hustled into the escape room followed by Emily.

It was only a four or five foot drop from the window to the roof of the garage. Arturo removed the window screen and let it drop. He climbed out of the window and landed lightly on the roof of the garage. Petie came next and then Emily. Before slipping down onto the roof Emily reached in and pulled the window shut. If they checked the prison room there would be no indication of how they escaped. They might waste time searching the second floor rooms.

The three crept over the ridge of the garage roof and slid down to the back. Arturo grabbed he edge of the roof and lowered his body down. He dropped lightly onto the ground.

"You next, Petie," Arturo said.

Petie slid over the edge of the roof while Emily grasped her hands. As she dangled above him Arturo grabbed her legs. "All right," he said, "let go."

Emily let go and Petie slid down into Arturo's arms and then onto the ground.

Emily came next, but without someone to support her from above, she let go of the edge of the roof and came down with a crash. Arturo broke her fall but lost his balance and the two of them tumbled to the ground.

"I'm sorry, Emily, I lost my balance."

"That's all right, Arturo, you're OK and I'm still in one piece."

In the meantime, Petie stood there trying to stifle a laughing spasm. "You both looked so funny, I wish I had a movie camera!"

"Petie," Emily said. "sometimes I wish I could kill you."

Then she stopped, thinking of all of the terrible things that had happened she felt chagrined and added, "I really didn't mean that Petie."

They looked around. There was nothing to indicate that their escape had been observed.

"Let's see what's in the garage," Emily said.

Cautiously Emily opened the rear entry door of the garage. All clear. In the corner of the garage next to the rear wall were the washer and dryer, and the gas-fired water heater she had noticed before. A door led from the garage to the kitchen and to the left of the door was a work bench with tools and things.

"I have to get the cassette. The man with the limp put it in the refrigerator. You two hide in the shrubbery behind the kitchen. If I get caught I'll scream my head off."

Addressing Arturo she said, "You and Petie run for the truck. If I create enough of a ruckus you should have time to get the motor started."

"We can't leave you here by yourself, Emily." Petie protested.

"You'll have to. There's no point in all of us getting caught. If you can escape you can try to get help. But don't worry, I'll be careful. Now, into the bushes the two of you, and keep your ears open." She handed her shoes to Petie.

XXV

Emily opened the door leading from the garage to the kitchen, just a crack. She could hear the television noise in the background. She pushed the door open. The kitchen was clear.

There was a blank wall to the left of the door and beyond that a doorway leading into the living room. Through the doorway she could see the backs of the two men in the living room as she sneaked by. They were still watching television.

This was a large kitchen with counters and cupboards and cooking facilities. Table and chairs took up a large part of the space. Beyond was the doorway leading into the dining room. To the left of the table was a door, probably to some kind of storage area. Emily, in her stocking feet moved noiselessly across the room.

She opened the freezer compartment of the refrigerator. There was the cassette! She picked it up and quietly closed the refrigerator door. Just then she heard the click, click of heels on the tile floor of the living room. By the rhythm of the clicks she knew it was the ugly one approaching!

She looked around. Nowhere to hide in the kitchen; if she moved through the doorway to the dining room she would undoubtedly be seen by the man watching TV.

The door behind the table, Emily pulled it open. Inside was a large pantry with shelves filled with canned goods! She squeezed into the pantry, leaving it open just a crack so she could see into the kitchen. Just in time, for at that moment the ugly one came into sight. From her limited view see the ugly one passed out of sight, but she heard him open the refrigerator, and heard the clink of one bottle of beer against another. The refrigerator door closed.

The ugly one started to leave, but then noticed the open crack in the pantry door. He turned back. Emily picked up a can. If he opened the door she would smash him on the head and run. Her heart was beating so loud and so she thought surely he would hear it. If she could knock him out she might be able to grab his gun, if he was carrying it on him. Emily held the can over her head, resolved to crash it onto his head with all of her might.

All of these thoughts raced through Emily's mind. If she did get his gun, what next? The man with the limp would surely hear the commotion and would come to investigate. Should she shoot it out with him? She had learned to shoot a rifle and a shotgun, but she had never even held a handgun in her hands.

The ugly one approached the pantry, but he only grunted, leaned over and pushed the pantry door; it shut, with a quiet ‘clump’.

Emily listened for his retreating heels. When she was sure the ugly one was gone, she sneaked out of the kitchen clutching the cassette tightly. At the back of the garage she signaled to Petie and Arturo to come over.

“What now?” asked Arturo.

“How long will it take you to start the truck?”

“I only hot wired my own Toyota once. I’d say somewhere between thirty seconds and two minutes. We could make a run for the truck, but there’s a window next to the driveway where the truck is parked. If they spot us they’ll shoot us dead before we can get it started.”

“Then we’ll have to create a diversion,” Emily said.

“What’s a diversion?” Arturo asked.

“A diversion is a distraction, it’s like . . . well, never mind. You’ll see what I mean in a few minutes. I hope.”

“Petie," Emily handed her the cassette, "here's the cassette; hide in the bushes where you can see through the kitchen window into the house. If you see anyone in there throw a stone at the back of the garage. Arturo, you come with me.”

In the garage Emily turned off the pilot light of the water heater. An orange colored electric extension cord, the kind used out of doors, for electric lawn mowers and the like was on the work bench. She picked up the extension cord and a knife.

“Arturo, see if you can drag the dryer away from the wall, and try to do it without making too much noise.”

While Arturo complied Emily stripped about six inches of the outer insulation from the extension cord, about six feet from the plug end. This exposed three wires, one black, one white and one bare copper. Emily stripped about three inches of the insulation from the black wire and this exposed numerous strands of shiny copper wire. Emily cut through the strands creating two ends which she then ruffled so that the wires of each end were just barely touching.

Next she cut off the plug at the far end of the extension cord and removed about three inches of the orange outer insulation. She then removed a half inch of insulation from the black and the white wires, exposing the strands of copper wire, and then bent the wires in opposite directions so that their ends were far apart. She plugged the altered extension into the electric outlet above the washing machine.

"What is that for?" Arturo asked.

"We're going to create an explosion. We'll let gas escape into the garage. The extension cord will be used to ignite it. We'll roll out the extension cord outside as far as it will go. When there's enough gas in the garage I'll touch the ends of the black and white wires together. That will make a spark here, where I've bared the wires and the spark will ignite the gas. Boom!"

Arturo had moved the dryer away from the wall and this exposed the flexible cable leading from the gas line to the dryer.

“Get a wrench from the work bench and disconnect the flex line from the gas line,” Emily ordered.

Arturo, having been brought up to believe that women shouldn’t do too much thinking and should respond to orders rather than give them was nonplused. He looked at beautiful, young Emily in wonderment!

"Arturo!" The second imperative prompted him into action. While Emily unraveled the orange extension cord out into the area behind the garage and as far as the bushes where Petie was waiting, Arturo disconnected the flex line. When Emily returned Arturo stood watching the gas line. The gas didn't come out with a hiss but with a heavy, quiet whisper.

"Get a hammer, there's one on the work bench. Stand here by the door where you can see me. I'll be at the edge of the bushes. Keep the door partially closed. I'll give it another three minutes. When I give you the signal, take the hammer, run into the garage and bang the side of it against the kitchen door three or four times. Then run like hell and close the door behind you."

Arturo no longer questioned Emily's right to give orders, he just nodded.

Emily returned to the bushes and kept a close eye on her watch. Three minutes. She decided to give it another minute or two and hoped that would be enough. . .

She signaled to Arturo. He disappeared. There were four muffled thumps and then Arturo ran from the garage, closing the door behind him.

Arturo was coughing. "Man," he said, "there's a lot of gas in that garage!"

From their vantage point in the bushes they saw the face of the ugly one peering through the kitchen window. Then the face disappeared.

"I'll give it five more seconds," Emily counted, "One-two-three-four-five."

Emily pressed the ends of the black and white wires together. There was a small spark in the wires, followed by an enormous explosion in the garage. The entry door to the garage was blown outward and completely shattered. The glass in the kitchen windows was shattered and blown outward. The entire garage was filled with smoke and flames and this had burst forth into the kitchen.

Petie said, “When you create a diversion, Emily, you create a diversion!”

“Quick,” Emily said, “we have to get out of here. You and Petie run ahead and get the truck started.”

As they passed by the rear of the garage smoke and flames billowed out through the doorway. Emily picked up the orange extension cord and yanked on it till it came loose. As she retrieved the cord she coiled it over one shoulder, leaving the hot, burned section at the end trailing on the ground.

Emily chased after Petie and Arturo, around the side of the garage and onto the concrete driveway.

Hindered by her high heels, she kicked off her shoes and kept running.

Then she stopped . . . ran back and picked them up. When Emily approached Petie was already in the truck and Arturo, with his feet on the driveway was under the dashboard. Emily threw the extension cord into the back of the truck.

The engine of the Toyota cranked over, and then there was the gentle purring of the engine.

"Move over," Emily said.

"I can drive," said Arturo.

"I said *move over,* Arturo."

Arturo knew better than to protest; he hopped up onto the seat beside Petie.

Emily thrust her shoes at Petie and said, "Hold these, Petie." Petie looked a little puzzled and perplexed. Why would Emily chase back after her shoes at a time like this?

Emily answered her unasked question, "They cost seventy-five dollars and they're almost brand new!"

Then she slid in behind the wheel and put the truck into gear, but Petie exclaimed, "Wait, there's a car coming!"

Just coming into the clearing was Rodriguez' black limousine.

"Turn off the motor," Emily ordered Arturo, "and everybody get down."

XXVI

Emily hadn't looked back since the explosion, but now, crouched in the truck she looked out and saw the garage and the back of the house burning furiously.

The limo rolled up the driveway and onto the grass by the front porch. Three men got out and ran up the front steps followed by the bulky Rodriguez who waddled along behind. He climbed laboriously up the steps and then stopped to catch his breath.

"Now Arturo," Emily said. Arturo responded and the Toyota purred back into action. Emily U-turned and sped down the driveway. Rodriguez, still on the front porch, gaped at the truck. When he saw who the occupants were he was at first dumbfounded, and then enraged. He shook a fat fist and shouted, *"Alto, alto!"* But Emily sped on.

Petie looking back said, "The garage and back of the house are completely on fire. If both of those men were in the garage then they're both dead."

When they were half way across the clearing they heard two shots but there was no sign of bullets.

"They were probably shooting from the bedroom," Arturo said, and he added, "Now they're running from the house."

As they were just leaving the clearing Petie observed, "They've started the limo."

On the upper stretch of the road Emily checked the speedometer; sixty miles per hour; that was as fast as they could go on this kind of road. As Emily slowed down to turn left into the first switchback a bullet twanged off the roof of the truck.

Racing down the next switchback they could see the limousine approaching in the opposite direction on the switchback above.

Shouting above the noise of the road Petie said, "The man behind the driver is shooting at us."

"If it's any consolation," Emily replied, "we're both doing sixty in opposite directions, so the shots he's firing are likely to fall way behind us."

They had now reached the rough, rocky part of the road and Emily slowed down to forty, still too fast for the condition of the road, but the necessity of flight demanded it.

"They're gaining on us." Arturo shouted. At the same instant a bullet tore through the back window and went out through the windshield.

They were in a bad situation and it was getting worse. They would have to so something and they would have to do it fast.

They were approaching the hairpin turn and Emily had to slow down even more. Ahead all that could be seen ahead was open space, with mountains far in the background and blue sky above.

"We're going to have to get out of the truck," she said. "The only reason they're not shooting at us now is that the road is too rough for them to take aim. But when we get into the next switchback it will be different. They'll be much closer to us and we'll be sitting ducks."

"When we get around the turn where they can't see us," she continued, "I'll stop the truck and turn it left so that it blocks the road completely. Then we'll get out of the truck and climb up into the underbrush. You might recall when we came up here that the road was steep at that point. When I park the truck across the road it might be in an unstable position. So all of us have to get out on the driver's side. Understood?"

Petie and Arturo nodded.

Emily right turned into the switchback, slammed on the brakes, and then deftly steered the truck so that it was at right angles to the road, and leaning precariously to the passenger side. Out of sight of their pursuers the three leapt from the truck. Agile Arturo scrambled up the embankment and lent a hand to Petie and Emily.

They couldn't see the limousine but they could hear the roar of its engine and the slap of the tires on the rocky road. The limo was approaching fast, too fast. Then it came into sight around the turn. Emily could clearly see de Jesus in the front passenger seat, with the window rolled down, and his right arm on the door, and his pistol in his hand.

At the same instant the driver of the limo saw the Toyota truck blocking the road. He instinctively sounded his horn and swerved left. The front fenders of the vehicles met. The impact caused the Toyota to topple over. The limousine went over the edge.

The limo went straight down the steep mountainside. There was a ripping sound as the vehicle rode over and ripped up the shrubbery. It looked as though the limo might roll on, right to the bottom of the mountain. But when it came to the next switch back it nose-dived onto the roadway. For less than a split second it was in a vertical position. Then it burst into flame and cartwheeled on down the mountainside, leaving small brush fires in its wake.

In the meantime the Toyota had continued to roll; over and over and over. When it came to the level area before the next switchback it gave a final lurch and ended in an upright position.

The three left their hiding position and started down the road. Arturo ran on ahead and picked up the extension cord which had fallen from the truck. Far below the limo had rolled over onto its side and had come to a stop. It was still burning.

Petie stopped, looked down and asked, "Do you think they're all dead Emily?"

Emily replied quietly, "Yes Petie, they're all dead."

Arturo stood staring at the truck. The roof was caved in about six inches. All of the glass was broken, except for jagged pieces around the frames. The hood was missing, and every square inch of the entire body was either bent, dented, scraped or otherwise deformed.

As Emily and Petie approached he turned to them and said, “Miracle of miracles! It must have rolled over twenty times but the motor is still running."

They stopped and listened. The engine of the Toyota was purring gently.

Emily tugged on the door handle, but the door was wedged in place and it wouldn’t budge.

On the passeneger side Arturo pulled on the door handle; the entire door crashed to the ground. Arturo picked it up and threw it into the back of the truck with the orange extension cord.

"OK Arturo," Emily said, "you can drive."

XXVII

Most of the broken glass had been scattered on the road as the truck made its unusual descent. They picked out the few remaining pieces. Emily dusted off the plaster residue on Petie's dress and they climbed into the truck.

Arturo eased the Toyota into gear, started up slowly and turned the vehicle down the road. Everything seemed to be working, so he speeded up a little; still no problem.

Suddenly Petie blurted out, "You were wrong, Emily, they aren't all dead!"

One hundred yards ahead a man staggered out from the shrubbery and onto the road. His face was spattered with blood.

"It's de Jesus!" Emily cried.

De Jesus, coming to his senses, turned and faced the oncoming truck; pistol in hand he moved to the center of the road. Arturo shouted to Emily and Petie, "Get down, both of you," and they complied.

De Jesus raised his hand and pointed his gun at the truck; Arturo pressed the accelerator to the floor and the Toyota leaped forward.

As the truck bore down on him de Jesus took aim. Just in time Arturo ducked down below the dashboard, leaving the truck to find its own way forward.

Three shots were fired in rapid succession. One thwacked into the cushion behind the driver's seat, inches above Arturo's head. Immediately there was a muffled crunch as the truck collided with de Jesus. The Toyota hesitated momentarily and then plunged onward.

Arturo brought the truck to a stop and looked backward. Fifty yards back de Jesus lay face down at the side of the road. "We'd better see if he's still alive." Arturo said.

"Wait here, Petie," Emily instructed.

"No," Petie protested, "I'm going with you."

"Then stay behind me."

They approached cautiously. De Jesus was obviously dead. His gun lay several yards away. Arturo picked it up by the trigger guard and tossed it into the bushes.

"We'd better get out of here," Emily said.

They returned to the truck and as they descended the switchbacks they smelled smoke from the many small fires the flaming limousine had started on its way down the mountainside. Near the bottom they passed the limousine, lying on its side and still smoldering. Petie hid her face in her hands.

"I don't want to look," she said. Emily stared impassively ahead.

As the Toyota turned onto the highway they all looked back at the scene. The smoldering limousine could be seen clearly as well as the path of small fires that led down to it. They couldn't see the mansion, but they could see flames rising above the tree tops; and heavy, billowing smoke.

"We have to get away from here as fast as we can, Arturo."

Arturo stepped on the accelerator. The truck leaped forward. With the hood of the truck missing, as well as the windshield, the roar of the engine was deafening. And as they increased their speed, road dust and insects added to their discomfort.

"I can't do much more than thirty miles an hour, Emily. It becomes too difficult to see after that."

"All right, Arturo, do the best you can. Petie and I will keep our eyes covered and our ears plugged. If you get to the point where you have to be relieved, I'll take over."

Arturo, with his Latin macho, wouldn't submit to that.

There were small groups of huts here and there on each side of the highway, but otherwise little sign of human habitation. The huts became more numerous, suggesting that there were nearing a town.

They had been driving for an hour when Arturo, bleary-eyed, announced, "We're here."

Emily and Petie sat up. Emily said, "We're where?"

"The sign on the road said. 'Quetico.' From what I can see of it, there's a hotel, and a bank, and a gas station."

"What I want first," Emily said, "is a telephone."

"There's probably one in the hotel."

"Then let's go there first."

Arturo parked in front while Emily and Petie went into the hotel. Curious passersby asked what had happened to the truck.

"It rolled over," Arturo said. That seemed to satisfy their curiosity.

Petie ran from the hotel. "Arturo, Emily can't communicate with the telephone operator."

Arturo soon conveyed to the operator that they wished to place a collect person to person call to Edward Gorman, at the American Embassy in Bogota.

A few minutes later a voice said, "This is Edward Gorman."

"Eddie, this is Emily."

"Thank God, Emily! Where are you?"

"We're in a little village named 'Quetico', other than that haven't a clue as to where we are."

Emily continued and briefly described the episode from the time of their abduction to the present.

Gorman was elated to hear that the most powerful drug dealer in Colombia was no more, but he warned Emily that the destruction of the limousine with dead bodies inside, and the destruction of the mansion by fire would not go unnoticed. By morning the Colombian army would be investigating, and it would be best if they were not in the immediate vicinity.

She was puzzled. "Aren't they in the same army as the Commandos?"

"Yes, but they carry out a different function. The Commandos carry out special assignments, a stretch between 'search and destroy' and 'hit and run.' The army in the area you're in have the occasional skirmish with the rebels, but there basic function is that of a police force. If they take you into custody they will interrogate you mercilessly and it might be weeks before we can arrange your release. In the meantime you might find it difficult to explain how you left behind a burned out limousine, a mansion destroyed by fire, and six dead bodies."

Emily explained the condition of the truck, that it was almost impossible to travel faster than thirty miles per hour.

"Well Emily, looking at my map I see there is another little town, a little bigger, about thirty-five miles from where you are. It's called Rumorosa. Do you think you can make it that far?"

"I guess we'll have to Eddie. I'll phone you when we get there."

“Get into the hotel there and keep a low profile.”

Emily conveyed Gorman’s statement about the army and their traveling plans to Arturo and Petie. “I thought we were almost home free; now we have to worry about being picked up by the army.” She added, "I'm going to drive Arturo, at least half way. So don't argue."

A weary one hour later they pulled into Rumorosa. Emily stopped at a gas station.

“Why are we stopping here, Emily? We don’t need gas and we don’t have any money anyway.”

“Wait here Arturo, and come with me Petie.”

In the privacy of the ladies bathroom of the gas station Emily removed two one hundred dollar bills from her money belt. She gave one of them to Petie, and they returned to the truck.

“Get rid of the truck, Arturo. And meet us at the hotel, it looks like it’s about two blocks down the street.”

By now Arturo was used to following Emily's orders without question. He put the truck in gear and drove away.

"Where to now, Emily?" Petie asked.

"First we have to get some Colombian pesos and then we'll meet Arturo at the hotel."

From the bank they returned to the hotel. Arturo was waiting in the lobby.

"What about the truck?" Emily asked.

"I parked it on one of the back streets, next to an automobile wrecking yard. No one will take notice of it there. I felt bad about abandoning it, Emily."

"I know, Arturo, the Toyota saved our lives."

Rooms were arranged for. They agreed to clean up and meet again in the lobby in half an hour. As always, Arturo was waiting for Emily and Petie when they returned.

"We have to get out of these dressy clothes," Emily said, "we look too conspicuous. You look all right, Arturo, except for your jacket." Emily peeled off some peso notes and handed them to Arturo. "Buy something conservative."

Arturo gaped at the money. "What did you do, rob the bank?"

"We spies have our methods," Petie giggled.

Across the street from the hotel, and one block down, was a store specializing in women's clothing. They bought beige-colored skirts and beige-colored blouses, and flat beige-colored shoes.

"With these clothes we can't possibly look conspicuous," Petie observed.

They also bought two conservatively patterned shawls. They seemed popular with the women they had seen on the street.

On the way back to the hotel they stopped into a drug store and bought three toothbrushes, two tubes of toothpaste and some toiletries.

Arturo was waiting for them in the lobby of the hotel. He displayed the conservative beige jacket he had purchased.

"Very nice, and we have a present for you, Arturo," Petie said.

Arturo's eyes brightened; Petie handed him a tooth brush and toothpaste.

If he was disappointed he didn't show it. He smiled and said, "Just what I've always hoped for!"

"Time for dinner," Emily said. "Let's change and we'll meet back here in fifteen minutes."

Fifteen minutes later, as always, Arturo was waiting in the lobby. He stood and observed, with approval, the change in the ladies attire. They were wearing their new clothes, and looked neat and presentable and not out of step with the dress of the local gentry.

"Before we do anything else I have to call Eddie."

There was a public telephone in the hotel lobby. When Gorman answered she said, "Hi Eddie, we made it to Rumorosa and we've checked into the hotel."

"All right, Emily, stay out of sight as much as you can. We don't travel at night because of the rebel activity. Besides that the Army has checkpoints every forty or fifty miles. They would undoubtedly be curious as to why a diplomatic vehicle was on the highway in a remote area at night. We'll leave here early and we should be in Rumorosa by about ten. In the meantime, be careful, and good luck."

It wasn't too reassuring, but at least help would soon be on the way.

The hotel restaurant was not elaborate, but it was clean and the food was good and hot. They were all tired and ate almost in silence.

"I think we all need a good night's rest," Emily said. And she was right. None of them had slept well the night before while in the custody of Rodriguez.

Emily said to Petie before they climbed into bed. "I think we're safe here." But as a precaution she took a straight-backed chair and wedged it under the knob of the entry door.

XXVIII

Just after eight there was a knock on their door. It was Arturo, wearing his new jacket. He looked neat and conservative.

“I think we had better check out before we do anything else,” Emily said. "Eddie was concerned that the army might be looking for us, and we wouldn’t want to have them catch us here in our rooms. Let’s pack up what little we have.”

There was no one at the reception desk when they went downstairs.

“We’ve already paid for our rooms so let’s just leave our room keys.”

In the restaurant Emily said, “Eddie told me the he would be leaving in the limousine early and he thought he would be here by ten. It’s just almost half past eight. By the time we finish breakfast we’ll still have an hour or more to kill. And we have to try to keep out of sight.”

“Maybe we could go shopping,” Petie piped up, and giggled. Shopping was Petie’s solution to most problems.

“This may sound funny,” Arturo said, “but looking out of the window, across the street I see a Catholic Church. I don’t mean to make slanderous remarks about the army, but it seems to me that the most unlikely place that soldiers would be hanging around would be a Catholic Church."

The street was wide with trees on a boulevard strip in the center and three traffic lanes on each side.

"Good thinking, Arturo," Emily said.

"Good thinking, Arturo," Petie mimicked, and gave him a squeeze on the arm.

After a breakfast of bacon and eggs they sipped quietly on delicious Colombian coffee and relaxed. They would soon be safely back at the Embassy and a feeling of euphoria was setting in.

But Arturo, ever alert, said, "Oh, Oh! We've got a problem. The Colombian army has arrived. They've pulled up in front of the hotel."

Emily looked out to see four soldiers alight from an army vehicle. "Let's get out of here."

Emily paid and they headed for the front exit of the restaurant.

"We'll leave separately, you first Arturo, I'll follow and Petie last. Walk down to the corner and head for the church."

"Cover your head with your shawl," Petie said to Emily.

They left the restaurant. There were few cars in Rumorosa but many pedestrians. The three blended easily with the walkers and crossed over the street without incident. In the church, Emily and Petie sat in the back pew. Several of the pews near the altar were occupied. They were surprised to see so many people in the church at this hour, nearing midmorning on a week day.

"I'll keep watch outside," Arturo said. He moved to the shadow of the doorway where he could not be seen from across the street.

A bus pulled up in front of the army vehicle and stopped at the corner. Rumorosa was too small a community to have its own bus service, so it must be a bus heading for Bogota. If they could get out of the church and over to the bus stop without being seen by the soldiers, but no, that wouldn't do, Gorman wouldn't know what had happened to them. And the soldiers might follow the bus and pick them up somewhere along the way.

Just then a funeral procession moved slowly down the street and pulled up in front of the church. The soldiers, seeing this, left their parking place in front of the hotel, drove quickly to the corner and made a U-turn. They pulled up to the curb in front of the funeral hearse.

Arturo hurried inside. "The soldiers are coming. We had better move up to the front and mix in with the other people."

"You find a place on the right side, Arturo. Petie and I will stay on the left."

Arturo sat down near the front beside three men. He looked like part of their group. Emily and Petie, with shawls over their heads, as was the custom, found a space a few rows from the front.

The church doors opened and the casket, on a wheeled platform, was pushed down the isle with mourners following. The casket was brought to a stop in front of the altar and the mourners took their places in the pews on either side.

A priest entered from a doorway to the left accompanied by two altar boys and faced the congregation, but he was looking beyond. Soldiers had entered. Two were marching down the center isle and one each on the side isles. They were scrutinizing the mourners as they passed.

"Quick Emily, kneel down and bow your head as though you were praying." Petie knelt down beside her.

When he came to the pew they were occupying the soldier stopped and looked closely at Emily. Emily's head was bowed and her rosy cheeks were mostly hidden by her shawl. Petie leaned over toward Emily and pretended to dry her tears with a Kleenex. At the same time she applied consoling pats on the back with the other hand. The soldier was satisfied that this must be a grieving relative and passed on.

The funeral Mass proceeded and this included a brief eulogy in Spanish. The only thing they could glean from the eulogy was that the deceased was a very nice lady. When the Mass was done the priest said some prayers over the casket and sprinkled it with holy water. The priest then passed by the casket and, preceded by one of the altar boys who was carrying a cross high in the air, and followed by the other, proceeded down the isle toward the entry. The casket was pushed along behind them. When they reached the entryway of the church the priest and altar boys stepped aside and allowed the casket to pass, followed by the mourners.

"It's nine-thirty. Eddie said he'd be here about ten. That gives us half an hour or so to wait." Emily and Petie resumed their places on the rear pew where they had stashed their bags of clothing .

"I'll check outside," Arturo said.

He came back moments later, concerned.

"The army vehicle is parked in front of the hotel. I think they're just watching the people leaving the church."

"Or they may be watching the hotel. They must know from the desk clerk that we were in the hotel last night. If they checked in the restaurant they'll know we had breakfast there, just minutes before they arrived."

"But if they were watching the hotel they wouldn't park right in front of it. I think they are more interested in the church." He added, "Despite what I said about soldiers not hanging around churches."

Arturo left to continue his watch on the soldiers. He returned a few minutes later.

"They've left. As far as I could see they headed straight out of town. But that could be a ruse. If they're suspicious of the church they could double back and try to catch us by surprise. If two come in through the back of the church and two through the front, we won't have any chance of evading them."

"I know you won't like this suggestion, but I think you should lie down under this end pew you're sitting on. The back goes right down to the floor so it is probably the best hiding place in the whole church. Stay there until Eddie arrives. If I see the soldiers coming I'll kneel in front of the altar and pretend I'm praying for the deceased."

Don't pretend, Arturo," Petie chided, "she was probably a very nice person and would appreciate your prayers." Petie always looked on the bright side.

Emily and Petie crawled under the pew. They settled on their backs, head to head so that they could communicate, by whispering if necessary. "Why did I ever become a spy?" Emily groaned.

"It was for the money," Petie said, "don't you remember?"

Petie paused and then asked, “What do you think they would do if they caught us, Emily?”

“I don’t think we shoud think about that, Petie.”

Half an hour later Arturo came back. "Hurry," he said, "the limo is here."

Emily and Petie slid out from under the pews and leaped to their feet. Emily dusted off Petie, and herself, and they hurried to the church entry.

There on the street, parked in front of the hotel was the Embassy limousine. They could see the Embassy medallion clearly on the driver's door.

They rushed out of the church. "Wait," Emily ordered, "we had better go singly, just in case someone is watching."

They hustled down the street to the intersection, as order by Emily - Petie first, Arturo second and Emily taking up the rear, again blending with other pedestrians. They crossed the street and turned toward the limousine. As they approached Gorman was just walking out of the hotel, looking worried.

He was elated when he saw them. "Emily! Petie! Arturo! I thought you had disappeared on us again. Quickly, get into the limo."

They were seated and the limo sped away.

XXIX

"I'll bring you up to date on what happened since you disappeared and then you can tell me about your experiences."

Eddie continued. "We knew within an hour that you had been kidnapped. The driver of a car behind the kidnapper's limousine jotted down the license number of the vehicle and reported it to the police. The driver of the taxi phoned his headquarters and they phoned the police. In the meantime, the abandoned taxi cab was blocking traffic at the start of rush hour."

"The police checked at your hotel and learned that you had, on more than one occasion, visited the American Embassy. They contacted the Embassy and we knew you had been snatched."

"The license number on the limo confirmed that it was owned by Rodriguez, considered to be the most evil and influential dealer in the cocaine industry. But Rodriguez had surrounded himself with a barricade of legal protections."

"The Ambassador was furious, not only at Rodriguez, but at himself for putting you in harm's way. He went right to the top, in Washington. Within a few hours it was confirmed that a raid would immediately be conducted on Rodriguez' headquarters using the same Commandos who had carried out the successful raid for us on the coca field."

"The only problem was that the Commandos were off on another mission and would not return until the next day. The raid had to be postponed."

"In the meantime you, Emily, phoned from Quetico and we knew you were safe, not as safe as we would like you to be, but at least you were not in the custody of Rodriguez."

"As it turned out the delay in deploying the Commandos was probably fortunate. If the raid had been carried out as originally decided, you would still have been in the custody of Rodriguez. The Commandos first objective was to see that you were safe and unharmed. They are very competent, as you know, but Rodriguez maintained a heavily armed camp, and who knows what the final outcome would have been?"

Emily, Petie and Arturo nodded appreciatively.

"By the time he raid was to be carried out on the Rodriguez headquarters we knew, from you, that he had been killed. This was relayed on to the Commandos just before their operation was to begin. And the Commandos made this known to Rodriguez' military establishment. A few shots were fired but the Rodriguez camp, caught completely by surprise and without their chief for guidance, yielded to reality and surrendered."

"But of even more importance, a wealth of information was captured. The names and locations of the other drug dealers, details about their operations, the location of their coca fields, and even more important, a list of government officials who were on the payroll and were providing information to the drug people. The drug people had so much money that bribery was their longest suit in evading arrest or prosecution."

"Did anything turn up about Montoya?" Emily asked. "Rodriguez told us he had hired him to raid the coca fields in Bolivia, using the pathogen he had stolen from us."

"There were complete details of his deal with Rodriguez. We contacted our Embassy in Bolivia and they have conferred with the police there. They have him in custody but they haven't decided whether to charge him there or ship him back to Colombia."

"They could charge him with entering their country with an illegal substance, but they aren't clear on whether the pathogen can be considered an illegal substance."

"If they send him back to Colombia then the Colombians have a problem. All that they have is that he is said to have robbed two Americans and a Mexican in Mexico. That puts us on the spot. We would have to reveal details of our jungle operation and Mexican officials would be upset. Moreover, the news would reach the American media and the whole world would find out what we were up to."

"Does that mean that Montoya will walk?" Emily asked.

"It looks that way, Emily. I know you must have some bad feelings about him after the way he abused you. But at least we would have the pathogen back. That brings up another legal point. If he's charged in Bolivia they'll have to retain the pathogen as evidence, and who knows when we would get it back, if ever?"

"Eddie," Arturo said, "as you know we had to abandon the Toyota truck. I felt bad about that. The Toyota was there to help us when we escaped from captivity. And it was the Toyota that sent Rodriguez' limousine over the edge and to its destruction. And, despite its battered condition, it got us as far as Rumorosa. Do you think it would be possible to bring it to the Embassy?"

"It has certainly played a big part in our work against the drug dealers, Arturo. You all, I mean, the three of you, were seen in the Toyota when you stopped at that gas station. That's why the soldiers were looking for you. It would be best, for the time being at least, if you were not associated in any way with the destruction of the mansion."

"Are we in trouble for burning it down?" Petie asked.

Emily said, "No we aren't, Petie; I think there may be some political considerations involved that we don't know about, and don't need to know about."

Gorman gave Emily an appreciative nod, "I'll ask the Ambassador about it Arturo. I'll recommend that we bring the Toyota to Bogota. Do you think will be driveable over that distance?"

“It wouldn’t be the most comfortable ride, but I think if you rigged up some kind of windshield it could be done.”

They were not on the best highway in Colombia. It had a gravel surface with numerous potholes and occasional washboard stretches. The limousine took them mostly in stride and kicked up an enormous cloud of dust as it sped along. They had driven for almost an hour when an army vehicle approached from the opposite direction. As they passed the army vehicle braked, U- turned and chased after the limousine. When they caught up the army officer in the front passenger seat signaled for them to pull over. The driver complied and the vehicles stopped in a cloud of dust.

Gorman turned and addressed his passengers. "Get as far back in the limo as you can, and sit on the floor, and don't get out of the limo unless I instruct you to."

With the exception of the windshield and the windows in the driver's compartment all of the other windows in the limousine were tinted so that nothing of the interior passenger area could be seen from outside.

Emily groaned, "We always seem to be on the verge of jumping out of the frying pan into the fire."

"Eddie," Arturo said.

"Yes, Arturo?"

"When I was keeping my eye on the soldiers, watching them from the church, a bus pulled up in front of where they were parked and took on passengers. I can't be sure but I think this is probably the same group of soldiers. They chose to ignore the bus and drove over and parked in front of the funeral procession that had just pulled up in front of the church. If you were to suggest that we may have left by bus they might accept that."

"Good suggestion, Arturo, I'll try it."

When they came to a stop the army vehicle pulled ahead. When the dust had cleared four soldiers jumped out, all of them armed. A lieutenant was in charge. By this time Gorman had stepped out of the front seat of the limousine. He was wearing a dark blue business suit and walked ahead to address the officer.

“Good morning Lieutenant.”

Gorman, with his upright, athletic bearing and easy gait commanded respect. The officer saluted. “Good morning, Sir, we’re looking for two American women and a Latino man.”

“I’m on the same quest myself, Lieutenant. We expected to meet with them at the hotel, but when we arrived the desk clerk advised us that they had left an hour earlier. The bus to Bogota had passed through town at about that time and he suggested that they may have taken the bus.”

“Ah yes, the bus. We thought it more likely that they were hiding, . . er, waiting in the church.” He said nothing more but it was obvious that Gorman had planted the question in his mind.

He sidled over to the front of the limousine and peered intently through the windshield. Seeing nothing, he turned and saluted Gorman. The soldiers climbed into their vehicle, made a U-turn and sped away.

"It worked like a charm, Arturo. The lieutenant recalled seeing the bus but, since you were not seen on the bus stop, decided that you were more likely in the church. I told him that I was looking for you too. He was aware of the kidnapping. Over an hour had passed since the bus left Rumorosa. The lieutenant decided that it would, by now, be out of his jurisdiction."

"Are there likely to be any more checks before we get to Bogota?" Emily asked.

"I don't think so. We're nearing the area where the Rodriguez' compound is located. The military will be busy there and won't have any reason to check the highway."

Gorman phoned the Embassy to inform them of their pending arrival, probably in two hours or so.

The surface of the road suddenly changed from gravel to smooth hardtop. The raspy grind of the gravel surface was replaced by the quiet hum of tires on a smooth asphalt surface.

The interest in conversation waned and the occupants of the limousine reflected on their own personal thoughts.

When the limousine pulled up to the Embassy the guard saluted and the gate swung open. The Ambassador, anticipating their arrival was waiting at the entry. He shook hands with all of them and with great enthusiasm.

"Congratulations to all of you. I wish I could fully express my admiration and respect. And let me add my apologies for allowing you to fall into harm's way. But come inside, we'll talk in my office."

XXX

When they were comfortably seated the Ambassador said, “First, let me tell you that the Bogota police were extremely upset because of your abduction. To have three foreign nationals kidnapped within the city boundaries was an embarrassment. They take great pride in providing a safe environment for visitors, despite the perils that exist elsewhere.”

“We delayed in reporting your escape from Rodriguez to the police until you were in the comparative safety of our limousine, under the able command of Mr. Gorman. Once that had been accomplished I was under obligation to make your escape known. I contacted Inspector Cambien of the Bogota Police Department and explained briefly what had occurred, and that you were, at the time of my call, on your way to the Embassy. He is here now. He has requested that each of you be available for questioning. And I should tell you that the Inspector is a friend of ours; you will not be grilled for information about your meeting with Rodriguez or any of the subsequent happenings. He is only interested in the kidnapping; and if he finds some way to take credit for your rescue, so be it.”

He buzzed his secretary. The door to his office opened and the Ambassador, in his diplomatic way said, “Allow me to introduce Inspector Cambien of the Bogota Police Department. Miss Emily Smith, Miss Petula Clarkeson, Mr. Arturo Martinez.” He added, "And, of course, you know Mr. Gorman.”

They shook hands all round and the Ambassador continued.

"The Inspector will want to talk to each of you separately. Why don't you go first, Miss Clarkeson, you can use the conference room."

Emily gave Petie a reassuring pat on the shoulder and she left with the Inspector.

Emily said, "I apologize again Ambassador for our casual dress. We had to dress like the natives in order to evade detection by the military."

"As I said before, Miss Smith, there are times in which practicality triumphs over decorum. Mr. Gorman gave me a brief summary of the activities you reported to him on the telephone. But I would like to hear the full story from you. Perhaps you don't fully realize how great a service you have performed for your country, and also for Colombia."

Gorman's secretary entered, carrying cups of coffee on a tray and slices of cake. She served it to each of them, accompanied by her charming smile. It was welcome as they had had nothing to eat since breakfast.

"I'll serve the others in the conference room," she said.

"Rodriguez was the most evil man in Colombia," the Ambassador continued, "and so powerful he was almost immune from the law."

Emily now gave a full account of their activities, how they were snatched from the taxi on their way to the Embassy and driven to the Rodriguez compound and held prisoner overnight. She described the meeting with Rodriguez and his plan to take over the cocaine industry.

The Ambassador, with raised eyebrows, addressed Gorman, "That's something we were not aware of."

"He probably planned to take over the heroin industry as well," Gorman added.

Emily went on to explain how they had duped de Jesus into leaving to return with Rodriguez.

Arturo repeated, almost verbatim, de Jesus' threat to shoot them all and watch them bleed to death. Gorman and the Ambassador shook their heads, almost in disbelief.

Emily went on to describe how they had penetrated the bedroom wall and escaped into the next bedroom and then to freedom behind the garage. She described how she had recovered the cassette of pathogen from the refrigerator in the kitchen and her near confrontation with the ugly one while hiding in the pantry; and the plan to create a diversion so that they could make their escape in the Toyota truck.

At this point Arturo interrupted. "Emily has used the word 'we' in describing what happened. But Emily did all of the planning. All that Petie and I did was help. If she hadn't figured out how to blow up the garage we never would have got away."

Arturo continued, "One man, we called him he ugly one, was a really evil person, but the other one, the man with the limp treated us fairly. We had mixed feelings about him. I'm sorry about him."

"Don't be, Arturo," Gorman said, "he was a dirty rat, just like the rest of them. He was one of Rodriguez' hired killers. The story is that four or five years ago he was sent to dispose of two of Rodriguez competitors. He shot both of them, but one, in a dying effort, pulled out a pistol and shot the killer in the knee. In return he received a hail of bullets. For the 'man with the limp' his career as a killer was over. Rodriguez made him a caretaker."

Emily asked, "Was the mansion destroyed?"

"Burned right to the ground, Emily," Gorman replied.

Emily continued, "We escaped in the Toyota but the limo was chasing after us. They were catching up and there was no way we could outrun them. I decided to block the road just beyond a hairpin turn. If we could get up into the underbrush we might be able to escape. As it turned out, when the limo came around the turn, the driver swerved left in order to avoid collision with the Toyota . . and the limo went over the edge."

"Please excuse me for interrupting again," Arturo said," but Emily is being very modest in describing the incident. She was aware of the danger to the limousine that would be created by blocking the road with the Toyota. The fact that the limo went over the edge was not a mere accident."

The Ambassador was spellbound. "In all of my years in the diplomatic service this is the most incredible event I have ever heard of."

Petie knocked on the door and entered. "You're next Arturo," she said.

When Arturo had left and Petie was seated the Ambassador continued.

"The three congressman who came to get information on your project are now on their way back to Washington. Fortunately, Mr. Gorman had spent much time discussing it with you and he was able to give the all of the information they wanted. In the meantime, Special Agent Musgrove arrived today from Los Angeles, and Mr. Armitage from Washington. I have set up appointments for you with them tomorrow."

"I'll look forward to seeing both of them," Emily said.

"I know you must be tired, Emily, after all of your harrowing experiences. When you've finished with Inspector Cambien, Eddie will show you to the rooms we have reserved for you. We were able to recover all of your luggage from the taxi company, so let's hope you can now enjoy some relaxation. And incidentally, we are holding a banquet in your honor on Friday. That will give you a few days to get your feet back on the ground."

Emily noticed the Ambassador had dropped the formal 'Miss Smith,' and was calling her 'Emily.'

XXXI

While Petie and Arturo were busy in the garden Emily met with Agent Musgrove. She had only one brief meeting with Musgrove in Los Angeles, but now, with his casual charm, he seemed almost like an old friend, someone from home.

"I'm very happy to know, Emily, that you came through such an ordeal unharmed."

They shook hands and exchanged smiles and Musgrove continued.

"My reason for coming to Bogota is to determine, if possible, whether the man now identified as 'de Jesus' was responsible for the massacre in Los Angeles. An autopsy will determine whether it was he who died in the auto crash, but we need your evidence for corroboration. My understanding is the you saw him running from the mansion and get into the limousine?"

"No. I didn't see that because I was driving and we were headed away from the mansion where the limousine had stopped. But when the limo came around the hairpin turn we were only thirty or forty feet away. De Jesus was in the front passenger seat with the window rolled down. His right arm was on the door and his pistol was in his hand. I saw him quite clearly."

"The report I have of the accident scene indicates that he was found face down on the road, close to where the limousine had passed through. His pistol was found in the shrubbery several feet away. To me that would indicate that he jumped from the limo just before it hit the road. Emily related what had actually happened.

"I'll have to enter this in my report, Emily," Musgrove said, "but we won't share this information with the local police. In any event, his pistol is on its way to the FBI lab in Washington. I believe tests will prove that the bullets in the massacre were from de Jesus' gun, and with the information we have from you, the Los Angeles Police Department will be able to close their file. Police departments hate to have dormant, open files."

"I suppose that would apply to Mark Sheldon as well?"

"Yes it would, Emily, and I understand that there was no 'Wanda', that Sheldon was probably trying to say 'Juan de Jesus'."

"That's what I thought I heard him say. When we were in the custody of Rodriguez he introduced him as 'de Jesus' and I knew immediately that he was 'Wanda.'

Emily continued. "Did you hear anything more from Kevin Johnson, he said he was doing his best to cooperate with you."

"Yes, I was impressed by Kevin. I asked him if he would be interested in joining the Bureau and received an enthusiastic response. He completed an application and I endorsed it with my personal recommendation. Perhaps we'll all meet in Washington some time. I understand you'll be spending some time there."

"I hadn't heard about that, Mr. Musgrove."

Musgrove replied, "I hope I didn't let a cat out of the bag." He added, "I need to talk with Clarkeson and Martinez."

"You'll find them in the garden. They're looking after the coca plants."

Emily and Musgrove shook hands again and Musgrove left.

Armitage was waiting in the library when Emily entered. He rose and shook hands. Armitage was thin. He had a thin face, slender build and thin hands. He wore a gray pinstriped suit and a pleasant smile. He looked near retirement age, and a little weary, and when he spoke, he spoke quietly.

"I'm very pleased to meet you Emily. You can't imagine what a hornet's nest you stirred up in Washington. Everyone was aghast after the tragedy in Los Angeles, but jubilant to learn of your escapades here, and the demise of Rodriguez. That's why I'm here. The DEA wants to greatly expand the operation and I am authorized to negotiate with the Colombian government with regard to a building site, equipment, personnel, security, and so forth. I'll want to go over some of this with you in detail within the next day or two."

Emily said, "Having seen a real coca field I have some new ideas regarding distribution, in fact Sir, about the whole operation."

"All right, Emily, Armitage said, "Please continue."

"There are probably thousands of coca fields in Colombia. The one which we raided was only approximately three acres in size. The method of distribution which we had devised, I realize now, was less than rudimentary. While it might be ten times as efficient as the use of herbicides, it would still take a Herculean effort to effect the virtual destruction of the coca growing industry."

Armitage nodded.

"When we were in Rodriguez' custody overnight I was able to do a lot of thinking. I came to the conclusion that we could probably improve our own method of dispersion by a factor of more that ten by pelletizing the pathogen, and, instead of scattering it from a low-flying airplane, firing it at the plants using shotguns."

Armitage said, "There is one question that will be of vital interest to the Colombians. Is there any danger that the pathogens you have produced could affect domestic crops adversely?"

"We tested it against corn, wheat, and rice and, of course, coffee," Emily said. "But they were not affected in any way. We could conduct additional tests here before proceeding."

"They would probably insist on that," Armitage said.

"You indicated that you and I would be meeting again in a day or two so I know you don't want to go into a lot of detail today, but just as domestic crops seem to be immune to our product, the coca plant, as we found throughout our experimentations, were much more susceptible, perhaps ten times as much.

I've compared this in my mind to the susceptibility of American Indians in the nineteenth century, to European diseases, such as small pox and tuberculosis. The Indians had no hereditary resistance to these diseases and in many instances whole tribes were devastated."

Armitage took a moment to mull over Emily's thoughts and then asked, "Anything else, Emily?"

"Yes Sir, as you know, from the outset of our program we concentrated on pathogens which would damage the coca plant 'above ground.' This would produce the most immediate negative results. And 'results' were essential if, I'm sorry to interject politics into this, if we were to receive continued funding. Because of this we chose to ignore what we all knew. By 'we' I mean, Mr. Andrews, Candejar and myself, that only plant viruses could bring about the total destruction of the cocaine industry. But it takes time to infect a coca field with viruses, a year, two, or even three years. But when the field is infected it is infected forever, it can never again produce a coca plant."

"We'll work on that when I get back to Washington." Anything else Emily?"

"Just one more thought, Sir. If America can send a man to the moon, and send those clever robots to Mars, America, if she had the will, could virtually wipe out the cocaine industry throughout the world."

"And the heroin industry?"

"*And* the heroin industry," Emily replied.

"Heroin is derived from the poppy plant. Could you produce a pathogen that would destroy the poppy plant?"

"I have no doubt that we could. In fact, the poppy is a much faster growing annual than the coca plant and it would be more susceptible to disease. And terrorist organizations rely heavily on funding from the heroin trade. Destruction of the poppy fields would strike them a crippling blow."

"The way you say it, Emily, as mind boggling as it seems, I think you're right."

Armitage paused, and then said, "You and Clarkeson and Martinez have been granted a two week furlough. You and I will talk again, Emily, and then you will be free to leave whenever you have finished with the Ambassador. The three of you are to report to my office in Washington on the fifteenth. Incidentally, when you phoned me from Puerto Vallarta you were naturally upset because of the breakdown in security that enabled de Jesus to track you. Rodriguez' records revealed that he had an informant in the DEA. Rodriguez knew almost as much about your operation as you did yourself. The informant has been arrested and charged and faces a lengthy prison term."

"We also learned that de Jesus had followed Candejar to Los Angeles. In fact, he was a passenger on the same flight. He stayed overnight in the same hotel as Candejar. We assume that he waited for him in the morning and followed him to your office."

"That means that I didn't bring on the tragedy by telling Sheldon about the meeting." Emily let out a sigh. "I'm much relieved. But what about Sheldon, how did he fit in?"

"Sheldon worked for the company that supplied the program that you had recently purchased from them. Being a con man, he spotted an opportunity to make a dishonest buck and moved in. We assume he crossed paths with de Jesus, tried to make a deal with him, and received a bullet in the back for his trouble."

He handed Emily one of his business cards.

"In the meantime I will be staying here to supervise the building and supply of the laboratory. Two Colombian biologists have been appointed to work here and I'll review the disks and your notes with them."

"Will Petie and Arturo and I be returning here?" Emily asked.

"I'm not just sure, Emily. After the way you have conducted yourselves here you are held in high regard by the DEA. They may have an alternate assignment for all of you."

Emily reflected and thought cynically, "We killed six men in less than ten minutes. For that we're held in high regard."

Armitage continued. "Your salary checks have been mailed and will have arrived when you reach home. I'll need a complete expense statement from you in Washington. I'm assuming you have sufficient funds left to carry on."

"Yes, I do sir. Other than air fares we haven't spent too much."

Emily paused, "And there's just one more thing that I have to ask. We are to be the guests of honor at a banquet to be held by the Ambassador on Friday. None of us has formal clothes."

"Buy what you need. On your expense account mark the items, 'pre-approved by Armitage.'

"Yes sir!" Emily gave him one of her most gracious smiles.

Nothing gladdens the hearts of women, and restores their spirit more than the prospect of an excursion into the land of feminine apparel, especially when the expenditure has been approved as a necessary expense. Besides, it gave Emily and Petie a feeling of being appreciated.

XXXII

At the banquet Emily was seated to the right of the Ambassador, then Arturo, Petie and Eddie Gorman. Champagne was served before desert and the Ambassador rose. Conversation became hushed.

The Ambassador addressed his guests. "I'm sure you are now all aware of the exploits of our three guests of honor. I told them on their safe return to the Embassy that in all of my years in the diplomatic service this was the most incredible event I had ever heard of. Unaided they annihilated the most evil drug dealer in all of Colombia. Colombia is in their debt, as is America."

The Ambassador raised his glass and said, "I propose a toast to Emily Smith, Petula Clarkeson and Arturo Martinez."

The guests rose. To the unrhythmic clink of glasses conversation was restored.

Emily rose. Guests again became quiet. To the guests she said, "There is one that has not been mentioned, and without whose help we would not have escaped, and would not have returned to safety. I'm speaking of the Toyota truck which served us so well. Without the help of the Toyota truck we would still be imprisoned by Rodriguez."

Emily raised her glass and said, "To the Toyota truck." The Ambassador and guests rose, glasses again 'clinked' accompanied by the approval of all.

The banquet was a success.

XXXIII

The limousine waited at the bottom of the steps. Beyond it, at the far side of the driveway sat the battered Toyota truck.

"We'll place it on a pedestal next to the flagpole. It will be a symbol of American ingenuity," The Ambassador said.

"And Mexican," Petie added.

Quinn came out of the Embassy and spoke quietly to the Ambassador. The Ambassador was obviously upset.

“I can’t believe it,” he said. “Inspector Cambien phoned to warn us the the Federal police have issued arrest warrants for our three guests. They are on their way over here to serve them.”

“On what charge?” Gorman asked.

“He didn’t say, probably about the destruction of the mansion, and the two dead bodies.”

“But we didn’t leave anything behind that would connect us with the fire.” Emily said.

“That’s not exactly correct,” Arturo said. “I left the orange extension cord in the bed of the truck. When the truck was brought back the cord wasn’t in it. It must be out there somewhere. Also, we were seen in the area.”

“Our flight leaves in forty-five minutes,” Emily said. “Can we make it to the airport before the police get here?”

“That would seem to be the best plan,” the Ambassador replied. “The police can’t arrest you while you’re in the

Embassy, but you would be virtual prisoners here." He added, "Your two friends won't attract attention, but with your blonde hair and fair complexion, if they're watching the airport, they'll spot you immediately."

Emily's complexion still had a rosy glow from her long exposure to the sun on the day they raided the coca fields.

"Eddie," Emily asked, "would you ask your secretary if I could borrow a wig and some makeup?"

Gorman returned minutes later with a dark- brown wig and a container of cosmetic cream.

"All right, quickly now," the Ambassador said as he shook hands with each of them, "into the limousine. Eddie will go with you."

They piled into the limo and it headed for the back gate of the Embassy; through back streets they drove without incident. As they approached the airport terminal Gorman instructed the driver to turn off into the parking lot. In the meantime, Emily had donned the wig and applied makeup to her face. With sunglasses on she looked like a different person.

The limo stopped in the parking lot. When they had removed their baggage Gorman instructed the driver to pick him up later at the terminal.

"You and Arturo go first, Petie. You look like a nice young couple." Arturo looked at Petie and smiled. "And either talk or pretend to talk," Emily added. "People look more natural when they're talking."

Petie and Arturo left, wheeling their baggage behind them.

"All right, Emily," Gorman said, "Let's go. If you see a policeman or anyone who looks like a detective move so that I'm screening you. I'll wait in line with you till you check your bag and get your boarding pass. And remember what you told Petie and Arturo, 'talk,' so you look like you're carrying on a conversation."

With Gorman towing Emily's bag they walked to the terminal. Emily felt like there were a thousand eyes peering at her. But she kept smiling and talking, and Gorman responded. There were policemen at each of the entry doors to the terminal. Although they viewed Emily closely they showed no reaction.

They entered the passenger line. Petie and Arturo were up ahead. They looked like an ordinary young couple.

Gorman turned and made a casual remark to the man in line behind them, allowing him to look around. There were security police nearby, but their attention was not directed at Emily and Gorman.

"I think we're OK, Emily," he said. And they were.

Gorman accompanied Emily to the boarding area. They shook hands and Gorman said, "I can't tell you how much I admire you, Emily."

Emily said, "The feeling is mutual, Eddie. I'll always think of you as one of my best friends."

In the airplane Petie and Arturo were already seated. Emily took the aisle seat beside them. The door of the airplane slammed shut, the engines were started and they taxied to the end of the runway.

With a roar the engines were put to full throttle and they moved down the runway, gaining speed.

Petie, in the window seat suddenly said, “Look! We’re being followed!”

Speeding along with the airplane, beyond the wing tip was a Jeep with four federal police aboard. One of them was standing and was waiving frantically to attract the attention of the pilot.

“If they stop us now,” Emily thought, “we may be here forever.”

The pilot either didn’t see him or chose to ignore him. The airplane moved faster and faster down the runway; the police vehicle was soon left behind and gave up the chase.

The 747 lifted its nose skyward. They were airborne! They were free!

Emily tugged off her wig and, with a twist of her head, gave her blonde hair a swirl.

Next stop: Dallas, Texas; and then . . .

on to Los Angeles!

END